Recruiting Murder

A Brown and McNeil Novel

by

Frank Lazarus

the Author of

The Murder Gambit & The Phenom

COPYRIGHT

DEDICATION

This book is dedicated to my partner, Deb, who loves and supports me and allows me endless hours to pursue my passion. I love and appreciate you, Deb.

BOOKS BY FRANK LAZARUS

The Phenom

The Murder Gambit

Recruiting Murder

April Fool

The Good, The Bad, & The Ugly: 103 First Dates

Is Anything Alright?

Part I

Chapter 1

May 2022

I have a knack!

I know many people have a knack. For some, it is finding trouble. For others, it's picking stocks. And yet others, it is March Madness Bracketology!

My knack? I have the ability to identify basketball talent in young men!

I never thought this would be a career. Like many short white kids growing up in Philadelphia, I played "schoolyard ball." I was OK, I guess, just about six to eight inches too short, and everything that went along with that, or did NOT!

But I played against many great ball players; some went on to college and NBA fame, and many others just remained schoolyard legends in the hood. I am an asterisk in those stories; every now and then, a local kid might remind me we played some decent ball, but not like they were playing at Haddington, Tustin, and other inter-city playgrounds where the names Chamberlain, Hazzard, Monroe, Rogers, Hightower, McCarter, Jones, and others became legends.

Doing anything we could to avoid doing homework, we sat around talking endlessly about the players we knew or saw playing with or against our heroes. Who has the potential to play in college? Who could get into college? How about the NBA?

It was easy to spot the shooters and scorers. However, I became convinced they were a dime a dozen and did not guarantee success at the next level.

No, the best basketball players had something special. I was determined to understand that combination of tangible talent with the very intangible "something special."

That became my knack!

Chapter 2

February 12th, 1975

It's 1975, I am talking to a family friend, Laura Atkins, a female reporter at the Boston Globe. She knew what a basketball junkie I was. "Goldy, you should come up and have lunch with me and Red; he owes me a lunch."

"Yeah, right, Red is going to have lunch with me, this schmuck from West Philly!"

"Red loves to talk basketball with everyone. I'll tell him you are a huge Celtics fan, and I have shared some of your writing with him. You might even convince him he drafted Dave Cowens because of you. I'm sure he'll do it."

"What the hell am I going to say to Red Auerbach."

"You don't need a script; just relax, will you, Goldy? You like Chinese food, don't you?"

A Jewish kid who didn't like Chinese? If you want to eat on Christmas Day, you better like Chinese!

A kid from West Philly who is a Celtics fan. As always with me, there's a story. I love making my life into stories; some of them are even OK stories. This one is fair. Remember, I am a short white kid who started loving basketball in the late fifties. Bob Cousy quickly became my idol, and once a Celtic fan, always a Celtics fan. The legend of my bank shot a la Sam Jones is well known in West Philly. Not very well known, I guess; there could be two people who have mentioned it in the last 30 years.

Rooting for the Celtics in Philly during the Wilt Chamberlain – Bill Russell wars was a bit like rooting for the Russians to get to the moon first.

It got worse for me, I rooted for Villanova while I was attending St. Joseph's. Always the contrarian.

"Of course, I'll come up; let me know when you've got a date. I assume it will include tickets to a game?"

"Press box with me; I'll be back to you."

"Thanks, Laura!"

Why was Laura so anxious for me to meet with Auerbach? First, she knew I was miserable selling life insurance. Hating people was not a good attribute for selling anything, but when it became obvious that my basketball career was ending, what else was I going to do? I considered teaching, but I was reminded that kids were people, too. Ditto with coaching. Wasn't there something I could do that did not involve people?

Secondly, and more importantly, Laura knew I had a knack. Over the last ten years, I would give Laura my predictions for the Top Ten NBA draft picks. I was never wrong, even though occasionally, the teams selecting were. Would they ever learn?

But Laura was even more impressed with another list - players not selected in the top twenty that would be all-stars within three years. I was right on eighty percent of those. These were the picks that Laura had shared with Auerbach.

Over the last five years, I have also taken an interest in high school players. Laura had given me the names of sportswriters she knew on the East Coast, and I had written to them all. They occasionally would send me clippings, box scores, and articles about local players. When I could, I would drive North to New York, South to DC, and go to many games right in Philly.

Who had time to sell life insurance?

Chapter 3

February 23rd, 1975

Laura said we were set for Saturday night, February 23rd. It was a night game, so I could fly up that day, stay over with her and her husband that night, and fly back Sunday. A bonus was that the Celtics were playing their division rival, the New York Knicks, who were challenging the Celtics for the division lead.

My eight AM flight out of Philadelphia was only slightly delayed, and I arrived and claimed my bag at Logan International at ten-forty-five. Laura was waiting at the curbside, and I jumped into her car. We were meeting Auerbach at noon, allowing plenty of time to get to Chinatown, barring no shutdown in the tunnel. She thought it was best to head right to Chinatown and kill time there rather than run the risk of being late.

We got to Chinatown and parked on Oxford Street, a block away from Wai Wai, Red's favorite in Boston. With a half hour to kill, we walked to the Chinatown Gate and through the Rose Kennedy Greenway before looping back to Wai Wai. We entered the restaurant and were greeted by an attractive Asian woman who asked, "Good afternoon. How may I help you?"

"We are here to meet Mr. Auerbach."

"Yes, Mr. Auerbach just arrived; this way, please."

There was nothing spectacular about this Chinese restaurant: two small rooms with six tables each and a large takeout counter in the rear of the front room. The walls are adorned with traditional Chinese artwork and calligraphy, while ornate lanterns hang from the ceiling, casting a warm and inviting glow throughout the space. The tables are set with crisp white linens and simple dishware, and the chairs are comfortable and stylish. The overall ambiance is casual and serene.

The host led us to the back dining room, and at the back was an alcove where Red Auerbach awaited. As we approached, Auerbach stood, hugged Laura, and extended his hand to me. Laura offered, "Red, meet Lenny Goldstein, whom you know by reputation anyway, and Lenny, meet Red Auerbach, whom you also know by reputation."

OK, I'm totally impressed by now. Laura does know Red Auerbach; a little piece of me thought I was being scammed up until now.

"Good flight in? "Red asked.

"Any flight I can walk off from is good for me, thanks. Thank you for lunching with us. I guess Laura told you what a fan I was."

"She did, and I look forward to discussing basketball, but first, if you both are OK with it, I'd like to order for the table. They'll bring plenty of food, and if there is anything you don't care for, there will be plenty you do. This place ain't like my favorite in DC, but it's the best I can find up here."

Laura and I looked at each other, shrugged, and said, "I'm fine with that," at the same time.

After asking the server to "Bring my usual," Auerbach started the conversation, "Laura always refers to you as Goldy, so OK, if I do? And call me Red, please."

"That's fine, Red!" I profoundly added.

"When did this passion for studying basketball players start?"

"When I was playing, I thought, of course, I would be the best player ever. I wanted to learn why some good players became great and how some great players became elite. It did not help me much; I couldn't overcome my physical limitations, but it became a passion of mine."

Wendy interjected, "Passion or obsession, Goldy?"

"Both, I guess!"

Auerbach asked, "Have you answered your own question, why is that some excel and go to that very special level of greatness?"

"The best example that we all know about is your own Dave Cowens. Most teams and scouts had Cowens as a late first-round or early second-round choice, but I loved Cowens, and I thought he should be a top-five pick. I think, based on my rating, you took him at number four. Any regrets?" I asked, knowing the answer.

"None at all, but Russell had played against Cowens and seconded your assessment. But what did you see in him?"

"The knock on Cowens was that he was just too small at six feet-nine to play center in the NBA, but he had what I very loosely define as IT. IT is that special factor that never shows up in the box score. It is an obsession with winning, or perhaps even more so, an obsession with NOT LOSING. Cowens spends more time scrambling on the floor for loose balls than he spends standing in the lane."

"Interesting! How is it that you can see IT?"

"Shooting and scoring have become too easy; everyone can do that, and everyone is getting better. The ability to create your shots is getting to be more important. But IT, I see in their eyes. It's a gut thing."

"Who do you like in this year's draft?"

"Trying to get some free advice, huh? The obvious are John Lucas, Quinn Buckner, Adrian Dantley, and Scott May. The not-so-obvious, and my sleepers are Robert Parrish, Mitch Kupchak, Earl Tatum, and a real long shot, Mike Dunleavy."

"So how would you like to work for the Celtics, Goldy? I'd create a position, Assistant Coach, Director of Scouting, I don't know, something!"

"Whoa, Red! I was expecting you might pick my brain, but I did not expect a job offer. I'd have to think about that. Thank you!"

"What's there to think about Goldy? This is your passion, and you'd be doing it full-time and getting paid for it," Laura interjected.

"I'd have to move to Boston and travel all the time; I don't know, Laur, it's just something I need to think about. I'll obviously give it serious consideration. On the surface, it does sound like my dream job."

Just then, three servers arrived with what appeared to be a dozen dishes, only finding room on the table for half of them. They left the others on trays.

"You expect another dozen or so people, Red?" Laura asked.

"Think it over, Goldy, no hurry; you've already given me a couple of kids to think about in this year's draft. You've got my private number; call if you have any questions. Let's eat!"

And we did! Sweet and Sour Soup, egg rolls, moo shu, lo mein, shrimp stir fry, spareribs, General Sao chicken, rice; I'm sure there was more. I hoped Red was paying for this; the meal might cost more than my plane tickets.

Small talk about the food, tonight's game, the 76ers, and Laura's recent articles occupied us in between bites of food. We ate for about forty-five minutes, when we all seemed to slow down at the same time.

"You want to take some of this food home, Laura? If not, they give it to a local soup kitchen."

"No thanks, Red"

No bill was ever presented; was I supposed to ask about it? I guessed not; this was Red's show.

As we stepped outside, I thanked him again for the meal and the job offer and said I would be in touch.

Auerbach looked at Laura and said, "Bring him down to the locker room after the game; give him the full Boston Garden experience," he winked at her. Inside joke!

Chapter 4

March 2nd, 1975

Did anyone ever say no to Red Auerbach?

A week later, I was still struggling with this decision. I realized that it was not the traveling so much as it was the fact that I'd be looking at a couple of hundred kids, studying their strengths and weaknesses, ranking them by position, and perhaps even interviewing them and their families, and *then*, the Celtics might only select one or two of them. They might not select any of them. It seemed like a lot of risk and limited reward. And besides, I was a Philly guy and didn't want to become a Bostonian. Was there a better way?

I thought there was, but if Red didn't go for it, the idea might be dead in the water.

I called Red's private number and got an answering machine. I left a message. A half-hour later, my office phone rang, "This is Lenny Goldstein."

"Please hold, Mr. Goldstein, I have Mr. Auerbach calling for you."

I gulped!

"Hey Goldy, how are you?"

"I'm good, Red, thanks. I wanted to talk out this scouting job thing if you have a few minutes?"

"Absolutely; what's on your mind?"

"OK, the main issue I have, and it seems to be it would be an issue for you also, is all the traveling, evaluating, interviewing, ranking these kids, and then you only pick one, possibly two of them. It seems you would be spending a lot of money, and I'd be spending a lot of time, to find those couple of kids."

"That's why I don't have a full-time scout now, Goldy, but I think the game is changing, and as more money comes into the game, there will be even greater demand to win, and thus, finding the best players would give us an advantage."

"I've been looking for a better solution and let me tell you what seems like a viable possibility; I start my own firm, and this firm would do what I am doing anyway, rank college prospects, but I would sell that list to teams that chose to subscribe to it. Naturally, I'd hope you would be my first client team. If you do it, others would follow, fearing that if you were doing it, they would be missing out on something."

"How's that help me, Goldy? Now I am looking at the same list as the Lakers and Knicks!"

"True, Red, but you and the Lakers will have different draft positions, different position needs, different strengths, and weaknesses. You would rarely be chasing the same prospect. And if you occasionally were, that's no different than where you are now. But you all will be working with better information than you are now, and for less than hiring your own full-time person for those one or two players a year.

"And, because you would be my first client and the Celtics hold a special place in my heart, I would do a special consultation with you pre-draft; we'd discuss your team's needs and tell you my best bets to fill those needs. I couldn't promise you that exclusive forever as I might want to offer that to other teams as an upgrade to their subscription."

"How much might you charge me or others for this subscription?"

"How much were you thinking of paying me to work for you full-time?"

"I was thinking $25,000 plus $5,000 for expenses."

"So, you were OK with a $30,000 expense; I'd want to make $30,000 plus $7,500 for expenses, so my thought was I would charge you and other teams $7,500 a year; I would need five teams to make my nut, but the risk would be on me to get those five teams. And you'd only spend twenty-five percent of what you were prepared to spend."

"That might work, Goldy; give me a week or so to think about it and run it by Mr. Brown. I like your thinking."

"Thanks, Red! This only works for me, though, if you're on board. I cannot cold call the other NBA teams and propose this idea, but if I can tell them, "The Celtics are already a customer," that's got some sizzle."

"I understand, but I think your reputation may precede you, Goldy; I have spoken with several other GMs and mentioned the work you do. I'll call you within the week, Goldy. Have a great day."

"Thanks, Red, you too."

I next called Laura Atkins as I thought I owed her an update. She was surprised but encouraged. She liked the plan and offered to call a couple of GMs to endorse my work.

Red called a week later; we had a deal, and a month later, Future Stars, LLC, was born.

Part 2

15

Chapter 5

February 2022

Forty-six years later, to say my business had changed would be a gross understatement.

No one could have predicted the growth of the NBA or the money now in professional and collegiate basketball. Most of the growth came from TV, cable, streaming, March Madness, Shoe Companies, and all the sponsorships and advertising.

Every team now had its own scouting department, but fifteen teams still found my modest fee of $1,000,000 per year worth spending to get a second opinion from the sport's most recognized authority on player evaluation.

In 1982, I expanded to evaluating high school talent and offered subscriptions to the colleges that lagged the NBA in having their own scouting departments. The larger programs, of course, added a person or two, and then all the schools were doing something, even if it was just subscribing to Future Stars. In 2019, sixty-three Division One schools were paying Future Stars $250,000 yearly, and fifteen Division Two schools were paying $50,000 yearly.

At the age of seventy, I had stepped back, and my son, Jason, and son-in-law, JJ, were running the business, but they let me hang around and occasionally allowed a suggestion or two. Fifteen more staff were involved with talent evaluation, marketing, and technology.

My initial contacts with the NBA teams were gone; even Red Auerbach passed away in 2006. But I was diligent in building relationships with their successors, and while some teams moved on, others came aboard. Danny Ainge, whom I first suggested to Red as a player in 1981, has been General Manager now for eighteen years. He was thinking of retiring and was mentoring coach Brad Stevens as his successor.

I also maintained the relationships locally with the 76ers, as well as the Lakers and the Brooklyn Nets. Duke, Villanova, and a handful of colleges still called me first, and some of the local scouts throughout the country had me on speed dial.

Like all businesses, technology had a major impact on our business, and we did not travel as much as streaming, social media, and YouTube brought the players to our desktops. We still felt the need to visit with many athletes and their families, but the first contact was almost always made remotely.

In addition to our basic subscription rankings, we offered the NBA teams optional services like player and team evaluations and personalized recommendations at an additional cost, of course.

I now spend most of my time at my Hilton Head Island, South Carolina home. I hated the snow with a passion, and while not beach weather year-round, it was suitable for golf. Thanks to Zoom technology, me and the kids could view footage of players and discuss their merits.

This morning, I'm sitting on my patio overlooking the Broad Creek. At nine in the morning, it was cloudless but only fifty-five degrees. It would get close to seventy by two o'clock, in time for my tee time at Harbourtown Golf Links.

My cell phone rang; I could see from the caller ID that it was Satchel Abney. Satchel and I go back forty years; he was one of the first introductions Laura Atkins made to me back in the day. He lived in Newport News and worked for the Richmond Free Press until his retirement. It was three years since I had made my last detour over to Newport News on my way North to Philly. I hoped he was not calling to tell me his wife had passed; when I last visited, she was receiving chemotherapy for breast cancer.

"Yo, my man, pots and pans; how you doing, Satch?" my typical greeting for Satchel.

"Not bad for an old man, Goldy; how about you?"

"Another day on this side of the dirt is all good, Satch; how is Shanelle doing?"

"Good, we hope; the doc says the cancer is in remission, her hair has grown back, and she's regained most of the weight she lost."

"I'm sure it's that fried chicken and mashed potatoes; give her my best. What's up, my friend?"

"I don't know, Goldy, but you know how you've been saying for the last ten years or so that no great players get overlooked these days with iPhones, social media, and YouTube? I went to a four-team tournament last weekend in Petersburg, and there was this kid playing for Greensville County High that I think is the best player I have seen in the last twenty-five years. When I got home, I tried to do some research on him and came up with very little. His stats are not overwhelming, but I think he's got that "it" you're always looking for.

"I called his coach, and he sent me a YouTube video; I am going to send it to you, but I thought I'd call you first. I know adding him to your rankings is no big deal, but otherwise, I think the kid will wind up working on the railroad there in Emporia."

"I'd be glad to look at the tape, Satch; you think he's worth a visit? What's his name, by the way?"

"You decide, Goldy, but if you do, let me know, and I'll try to connect with you. His name is Lincoln Anderson."

"Sounds good, Satch; I'll let you know and give my best to Shanelle."

Ten minutes later, I had the forty-five-minute video. This team video did not focus exclusively on the Anderson kid, as many self-promoting videos did. After watching it for the third time, I agreed with Satch's assessment; Lincoln Anderson certainly had "it."

A six-hour drive and an overnight stay in beautiful downtown Emporia, Virginia? Am I being punished for something?

Chapter 6

February 15th, 2022, Emporia, VA

Emporia was best known for having an exit off Route I-95 and was a frequent first or second-night stop for travelers heading North from Florida.

Greensville High was playing Friday night at home. For me, it was a straight-up drive I-95 from Hilton Head. It was a shorter drive for Satchel Abney, who would probably hit Route 58 somewhere and travel due West to Emporia from Newport News.

I booked us two rooms at the Fairfield Inn right off the I-95 Exit. I told Satch I would try to be there by four o'clock and we could have dinner at five, plenty of time for the seven o'clock tip-off.

Finding somewhere to eat along I-95 was always a challenge if you wanted anything other than Cracker Barrel or even faster food. Sensing I might regret it, I asked Satch to make that decision.

My drive North was uneventful, with only a minor construction slowdown as I approached the Emporia exit. I arrived at three-fifty, and my room was ready. Fifteen minutes later, I got a text message from Satch that he had just checked in. We agreed to meet in the lobby at five.

Satch offered me a choice of Cracker Barrel or Home Plate, a small local diner ten minutes north on Route 301. Since Satch knew I only did CB for breakfast, I assumed he had a strong preference for this Home Plate place.

We climbed into my new Lexus GX460, and Satch immediately asked, "Whoa! Another new car?"

"Yeah, who knows how much longer I'll be able to deduct it for business?"

Ten minutes later, we pulled into the parking lot of this inauspicious eatery. We entered, and this place lived up to expectations, and I do not mean that in a flattering way. Grease, I assumed, was the specialty of the house. We were told we could sit wherever we wanted; under my breath, I thought, *does that include Cracker Barrel?* Let's see; there were four booths, one occupied, a counter with four stools, two occupied, and two small tables between the two. I would explain the décor, but there wasn't any.

I said to Satch, "Let's do the booth by the window so I can watch my car. I assume you have eaten here before?"

"Several times; just do the rib platter, and you'll be fine."

I did, and I was!

Forty-five minutes later, we were back in the car heading South to Greensville High. Satch knew I wanted to be early, pick out my preferred seat, and watch warmups. We parked at six-twenty, I paid five dollars for each ticket, and I climbed the five rows of collapsible stands at center court.

The mundane atmosphere was as expected. I quickly understood how a kid could get overlooked here; no one other than students and families would venture into the boonies here in Southern Virginia.

Both teams were on the court warming up. "Who am I looking at, Satch?"

"Number 23"

"I'm going to take notes on my laptop; you'll take the video. We'll upload both so Jason and JJ can review over the weekend."

I started a new document in my 2017 High School Seniors folder.

2/15/2021

Greensville County High School, Emporia, Virginia

#23, Lincoln Anderson, Greensville High School

GHS Greensville High School

SC Stony Creek

LA Lincoln Anderson

Anderson was referred to me by Satchel Abney, who has seen him play two games.

At first sight, the kid is about 6'5", lean but well-built. Muscular, but not excessively.

During practice, he is well-focused, and his movements and shots are purposeful. Occasionally chats with a teammate, but not just standing around, shooting the breeze. A POSITIVE!

As I had asked, Satch took video for about five minutes of practice. Unlike the YouTube video, Satch would focus only on Anderson, with and without the ball.

Practice ended, and the teams returned to their locker rooms. They would return at six-fifty, run a lay-up line, take a few shots, and the game would begin. We sat on the visitors' side of the gym with about twenty-five of the players' parents. They were from Stony Creek High, twenty-five miles North of Emporia. The Home team's stands were filled to about fifty percent of capacity; I estimated about a hundred spectators in all. I did not notice any other college recruiters.

The game started, and both teams wanted to run. The opening tip went to Anderson, who drove down the lane and, at the last second, dropped the ball for his teammate, who laid it in.

At the end of the first quarter, Greensville led 15-11, and I updated my notes:

First Q, LA scores six points; probably could have had twelve. He is a dominant player but totally unselfish. Being from the boonies and not having spectacular stats, I see why he did not draw any attention. He has a complete game, is an excellent D player, has court intelligence, and good movement with and without the ball.

The rest of the game went much the same. Greensville added to their lead, and with five minutes remaining in the game, with the score 55-41, Anderson came out of the game. I was certain he was done unless Stony Creek made a spectacular comeback. Final update in my notes:

GHS won; LA scored eighteen points on twelve shots. Ten rebounds, six assists, three steals, and three blocked shots. If he wasn't so unselfish, he might have doubled his points. Satch was right; this kid is a player.

As I closed my laptop, Satch asks me, "Whatta ya think, Goldy?"

"I think that you are absolutely right about the kid, Satch. You can email me the video, and I'll send it along to Jason and JJ along with my notes. I'm sure they'll agree to add him to our final rankings that we'll publish on March 15th, but you know many colleges do the bulk of their recruiting off our pre-season rankings. You were thinking or hoping he might yet get recruited?"

"Hoping, yes! No chance?"

"Let's see if we can catch him or his parents after the game and maybe meet with them in the morning. Find out his plans or whatever we can."

It seemed like the parents just hung around in the stands or on the court, waiting for the players to come and fetch them. A few of the younger siblings were out on the court, either shooting or dribbling, which no one seemed to discourage.

The players came out, usually in twosomes, then splitting to go to their respective families. We spotted Anderson and walked towards him. Many of the parents patted him on the shoulder, offering, "Great game, Linc." We got to him just as his parents and two siblings did. We stood by while they greeted him, and when they broke off, I stepped up. "Lincoln Anderson? Might I assume you are Lincoln's parents?"

"You may, but who are you?"

"Forgive me, please; my name is Leonard Goldstein, and this is my associate, Satchel Abney. Might we have just a minute?"

"I guess so; I'm Lincoln's father, Dwight, my wife, Estelle, and our kids, Dominique and Tawana. You seem to know Lincoln already. What's this about?"

Handing him my business card, I said, "My firm is Future Stars, and we evaluate basketball talent and work with many college and NBA teams. My associate here, Satchel, had seen your son play and asked me if I might come down and take a look. I am hoping that we might sit down with y'all sometime tomorrow morning, if possible, and discuss Lincoln's future."

"I'm not sure how much we might be able to tell you about that, but we would be glad to have you at the house in the morning, say at nine, OK?"

"That would be great. Let me get your address. Lincoln, you played a great game, congratulations."

We got the address, shook hands, and I said, "We look forward to seeing you in the morning; thank you again."

We all walked out together and separated in the parking lot.

"One drink at the hotel bar, Satch? After that, I'll get the video and notes off to the kids. I hope one of them can review it tonight or early in the morning."

"Sure, a brandy will help me sleep."

Ten minutes later, Satch had his brandy, and I opted for a Macallan Twelve, neat.

"So, boss, what do you think?"

"I like the kid a lot, Satch, but with only two weeks left in the season, graduation in June, and no idea about his grades, SATs, or his future plans, I'd say we are on a fact-finding mission tomorrow. You agree?"

"I guess so, but I'd hate to see this kid's talent end here in Emporia, Virginia in two weeks."

"Take it one step at a time, my friend, L'chaim!"

Chapter 7

I got up early Saturday morning and went down to the lobby for coffee with my laptop. I put my overnight bag in the car and wanted to review my notes and the video of last night's game.

I had heard from my son and son-in-law, and they both agreed that Lincoln Anderson needed to be high up on our list. They liked him in the top ten at either guard or forward. I thought he had another two to three inches of growth left in him, and forward might be his better position. But he was a great ball handler and shooting range, so the guard position was not out of the question.

Satchel showed his face at eight-thirty, carrying his bag.

"You gonna grab a cup of coffee for the road?" I asked him.

"Please, only take me a minute."

It took him three, as he first had to decide which coffee and then fix his cream and sugar like a barista. Eventually, he was ready, and we walked out to my car.

"Why don't we go in my car, and I'll bring you back to yours later? I saw a Dunkin Donuts just off I-95, and we can pick up some Munchkins. "Let's go!"

We found the Anderson home at eight-fifty-five and parked. It was a modest-sized community of townhouses I estimated to be fifteen or so years old. The homes and lawns looked well-kept, and many had bikes, Hot Wheels, and other assorted toys outside, suggesting some young families lived there.

Dwight Anderson must have been watching for us as he stepped out of the house as we approached. He offered a handshake, and we followed him into the house. Lincoln was in the living room and greeted us.

The living room was modestly furnished and quite cozy. It reflects their simple yet tasteful style. The room has a warm and inviting feel to it, with a comfortable couch and a few chairs arranged around a coffee table. The walls are painted soft beige, creating a neutral background for the various decorative elements in the room. A framed family portrait hangs on one of the walls, while a few art pieces and photographs are displayed on the shelves. Although it's not a large space, this living room is where the family enjoys relaxing.

Dwight said, "We thought we'd sit out on the back deck and enjoy this crisp morning."

Estelle Anderson was in the kitchen, which led to the outside deck. "Good morning, gentlemen; I'm bringing out some coffee; if you prefer tea, let me know. I'm seeing those Munchkins, so thank you."

We all got settled outside with coffee. The backyard was small but had a vegetable garden in one corner and a flower garden along one fence. Not a whole lot in bloom in mid-February.

"Thank you for seeing us this morning, Mr. and Mrs. Anderson and Lincoln. Again, nice game last night, Lincoln."

"Please call us Dwight and Estelle," Dwight suggested.

"OK, if you'll feel free to call him Satchel, and with me, you get a choice; I respond to both Lenny and Goldy."

Dwight said, "I did some research on you this morning, looked at your website, and googled you. It appears you have a big-time operation and are very well regarded. Just what again are you doing here with us?"

"As I may have mentioned yesterday, Satchel here saw Lincoln play a couple of times and was very impressed. He asked me if Lincoln was on our radar, and I told him he was not. He sent me a video, and here we are. So, I guess my first question would be, what are your plans after graduation, Lincoln?"

"My dad thinks he can get a job at the railroad. He's a maintenance supervisor there, and they always need people."

"No plans then for college or basketball?"

Dwight said, "We have encouraged Lincoln to apply to college, perhaps the nearby Community College, but as yet, he has not agreed to it."

"College is expensive, and since I'm not certain what I want to do, why spend the money?"

Estelle added, "We are trying to convince him that college will give him some options; he doesn't need to know right now what he may want to do for a career. We have some savings and can make Community College work."

I said, "Let me be honest with you nice folks; Satch and I, and now my son and son-in-law who run the business, all agree that Lincoln can play in college. We publish our final rankings of high school seniors in two weeks, and we will be adding Lincoln with a very high rating. Many schools, of course, have already filled their scholarship spots, but some others will see this ranking and ask, "Who's this kid?

"So, let me ask, how are your grades, and have you taken the SATs? And, if money were no object, would you consider college, and where might you want to go? Not a specific college, but a region? You want to be close to home, Florida, West Coast, East Coast?"

They all looked at each other, then at me and Satch. I may have overwhelmed them, but that is not a bad thing.

"Are you saying that you think Lincoln could get a scholarship to play basketball?" Dwight wanted to know.

Lincoln said, "My grades are OK, not spectacular, B's and C's. The school encouraged us to take the SATs, and I had a 1,125; they told me it was OK, again, not great. And if I had a choice, I'd like to stay close to home so my family could see me play."

I said, "Look, I am not a recruiter for any college, but I can tell you that you have the talent to play college ball. Your grades and SATs are fine, and with our ranking, there will definitely be interest. You may need to wait a year or perhaps start school and redshirt a year. We only have this one video that Satch filmed yesterday, and not much time for anyone to come and see you play. If you wanted to play in Philadelphia, I know I could get you into two or three schools on a phone call, but

I've got another hunch for somewhere closer. Might be a longshot, so I won't say anymore."

Estelle said, "So what happens now?"

"We finish our Munchkins, perhaps have another cup of coffee, enjoy this lovely morning, and let me do my thing. How about if I call you, Dwight, early next week after I play my hunch? Meanwhile, Lincoln, ask your coach if you can take a few more shots in the next couple of games so your stats will be better. And if he has someone who can take video, not of the game, but of YOU, that would be great. If not, perhaps Satch here can make another trip."

Dwight replied, "We cannot thank you enough, both of you. This is just incredible, something we could not have dreamed about a week ago."

"No need to thank us just yet; when we get this done, you can thank Satch here."

We all relaxed and talked about families; they asked me a lot of questions about my business and the players I'd met. I don't often need to get involved like this as the rankings and teams usually speak for themselves, but helping a family like this still gives me the chills.

A half-hour later, and after hugs and more tears, Satch and I are headed back to the hotel.

"What this hunch, boss?"

"I first need to stop and buy some underwear; I am heading up to Richmond."

Chapter 8

February 17th, 2022, Richmond, Va

Richmond Commonwealth University was in the Southwest section of Richmond and was not known to be a basketball powerhouse. In fact, in Richmond, they were the little sisters of Virginia Commonwealth University. But they played in the competitive Colonial Athletic Association, a conference that sent George Mason and Virginia Commonwealth to the Final Four.

But I wasn't headed there because of their rich basketball tradition, but because I believed their coach, Vince Blackwell, was one of the more progressive and innovative coaches in college basketball. Disappointingly, RCU was not a client of Future Stars, and I had only spoken with Blackwell once, three years ago, when he rejected my sales appeal to subscribe to Future Stars.

I confirmed that he was scheduled to be in his office but decided not to call for an appointment, choosing not to give him the chance to decline. I thought if he knew I traveled all the way from Philadelphia to meet with him, he'd give me a mercy meeting. I would keep my fingers crossed.

Richmond was an hour and a half from Emporia, but I made the trip yesterday and stayed at the center city Downtown Marriott Hotel. That allowed me to walk over to the Tobacco Company, one of my favorite places to dine in Richmond.

It was ten o'clock when I entered the offices of the Athletic Department at RCU and found the basketball offices. I was greeted by the receptionist, who asked, "May I help you, sir?"

"Yes, I am here to see Coach Blackwell."

"Do you have an appointment?"

"No, I do not."

"He's on the phone right now; may I ask your name and your business with the Coach?"

Handing her my card, I said, "Certainly, I am Leonard Goldstein of Future Stars, and I am here to tell the Coach I have a prospect for him."

"Please have a seat; when he is off the call, I'll let him know you are here."

"Come on in, Len, have a seat," Blackwell said as he stood and offered his hand. "I do not believe we have met before, have we?"

"We have not, and I sincerely appreciate your seeing me without an appointment. I'll be as brief as possible, Coach."

"No problem, but I still do not have a budget for Future Stars!"

"Actually, I am here for what I believe is a tremendous opportunity for you. I need to give you a bit of background. A week ago, I received a call from an associate of mine, and he told me about a high school senior playing in Southern Virginia. He asked me if the kid was on our radar and, if so, where he might be ranked. We never heard of the kid. He sent me a video, and the short story is that I just came from seeing him Friday night and met with him and his parents on Saturday.

"This kid has never been approached by anyone, Coach. He was planning to get a job on the railroad, like his dad. Our final rankings will be published in two weeks, and our team at Future Stars agrees to have him as a top ten, maybe even top five, prospect at either guard or forward."

"And what does this mean to me? I am not a subscriber to Future Stars?"

"We are not agents, Coach; I just told you what my university clients will learn in two weeks."

"Why me?"

"A couple of reasons: first, the kid would like to be in this area so his family might be able to see him play, and second, even though you are not a client, I have great respect for the job you are doing here. I think you would be a great coach for him, and he would be a player that might transform your program. I believe he is that good."

"What are you suggesting, Len? What is your or his next step?"

"Best case? I'm going to email you a video we took of him last Friday. If you are interested, and I am sure you will be, I hope you will go see him play; he only has three games left on his schedule. If you do that, I believe this will take its course. If you pass on him, I'll have this discussion with VCU and William & Mary. When our report comes out in two weeks, I believe the kid will have many other options. If he did not want to remain local, I know three schools in Philly that would have signed him sight unseen, on my say-so."

"You like the kid that much, huh, Len?"

"I do! I told the kid's parents, oh, I'm sorry; his name is Lincoln Anderson. I told his parents I'd give them some feedback early this week. If you are not going to pursue this, please let me know. I need to buy some more underwear if I'm going to be in Virginia for another day or two. One thing I should tell you is that his stats are not overly impressive. The kid has a complete game, and he's totally unselfish. He could easily double his per-game scoring average."

"That's reasonable, Len; I'll call you tonight after I've looked at the tape. Here's my card with the email address. I appreciate the visit and consideration. Safe travels back to Philly!"

"Thanks again for making time, Coach; I look forward to hearing from you."

I stood, we shook hands, and I believed with all my heart that this hunch of mine would pay off.

Chapter 9

March 15th, 2022

Tyler Longenecker first came to the attention of Future Stars when he was a sixteen-year-old at Beaver Country Day School in the Boston suburb of Brookline.

If I didn't tell you before, we pretty much ignored the McDonald's All-Americans and the Top Twenty high school stars over the last twenty years or so. They were heavily scouted, and there weren't many surprises. We, of course, needed to rank them, so we would watch tape and, every now and then, go to a game or two. Our focus would be on the other two hundred to three hundred high school prospects.

Tyler Longenecker was one of those Top Twenty prospects, and by the time he was a senior at Beaver, he had grown to six feet, seven inches. He could play any position and had good range, shooting forty-five percent from three-point range. He would be a forward in college.

It was rumored that he had received over a hundred scholarship offers. Jason thought the kid had "it," but JJ and I were still undecided. With or without "it," we would rank him a Top Ten prospect.

Late March was beautiful on Hilton Head; the temperatures would be in the 60s and 70s, which I much preferred to the 90s we'd have all summer. And the Island was not nearly as crowded as it would get when the tourists overran us in the summer.

I was out for a bike ride this morning when my cell phone rang. I glimpsed and saw it was Coach O, the iconic Pat O'Shea, longtime coach at Duke University. O'Shea was one of my first clients when I expanded into ranking high school talent, and we had become good friends over the years.

I pulled over, got off my bike, and sat on a nearby bench, "Hey, Patrick, good morning!"

"Morning, Goldy. Am I interrupting your nap?"

"Nope, just out for a bike ride and could use the break. What's up?"

"I just thought I'd check in and see what you may have heard about Tyler Longenecker; any decision there as yet?"

"I suspect when he decides, we'll all hear about it, but no, no decision yet. My sources tell me it's between three schools: you guys, Harvard, and Villanova. His dad is pushing for Harvard, so if he ever joins his law firm, he'll have the Harvard pedigree, and his mother fell in love with Jay Wright, so that kept Villanova in the mix. Tyler himself seems to favor you folks. Are you still holding a scholarship for him?"

"Of course, but I got one kid who's in limbo between Miami and us; I hate to keep the kid hanging."

"May I ask his name?"

"Sure, Noah Walker from Silver Springs, Maryland."

"Yeah, I'd wait for Longenecker, O! Why don't you come on down for a visit; we'll get some golf in?"

"I might just do that; I'll get back to you, Goldy. And let me know if you hear anything on Longenecker."

"Will do, good luck!"

Two days later, Longenecker announced he would be attending Duke University in the Fall. I learned it watching "Get Up" on ESPN.

Part 3

Chapter 10

June 10, 2022, Brookline, Massachusetts

Three months later, Beaver Country Day School held its commencement ceremony at the Charles River Country Club in nearby Newton.

It is a gorgeous day in the Boston area! The sun is shining brightly, and a gentle breeze is blowing through the air. The trees are bursting with new leaves, and the flowers are in full bloom, adding vibrant colors to the landscape. It's the perfect day to take a stroll along the Charles River, visit one of the city's many parks, or have a school graduation. The temperature is right, not too hot or cold, making it a comfortable day to enjoy the outdoors.

Everyone was glad the ceremony could be held outdoors.

The ceremony started promptly at eleven o'clock with the procession of the hundred and eight graduates. It appears they had found a way to recognize each of the hundred-and-eight students with some Special Achievement. God Forbid they may have missed one or two.

After diplomas were awarded and the students marched out, they all moved inside to the main ballroom for a celebratory luncheon for graduates and their guests. Luncheon speeches were held to a minimum.

That night, three of the parents had arranged for a student-only party at The Country Club in Brookline. Massachusetts law allowed for those under the age of twenty-one to be served on private premises, but all had agreed to limit that to beer and wine. Each student received three drink tickets. There was a rumor that some fake tickets were available for purchase on Tribel. There would be six parent chaperones, three security guards, and two bartenders, all monitoring the drinking situation. Parents were urged not to allow their children to drive to the party.

The theme for the party was "The Class of 2021 Goes to the Movies," and the students and parents had gone all out decorating the party room. Each of the students would receive their own personalized "Oscar," and each was featured in a poster of their favorite movie character. They would all be photographed arriving on the Red Carpet and being interviewed by Class President Kelly "Couric" Reynolds. Several students arrived in stretch limos.

Tyler Longenecker came with his girlfriend, Debbie Gibson, but they agreed in advance that they would both spend time with their own friends; for Tyler, that meant Nathan Friedlander, Billy Bender, and Sheldon Warner. The guys were fully loaded for the last and biggest blowout of their high school lives. Vodka, pot, roofies, and some Tranq ought to make for some excitement.

By 9:30, the party was in full swing. The DJ had been prepped about the Movie theme and interjected some old favorites like Footloose, Flashdance, Old Time Rock and Roll, and The Time of My Life from Dirty Dancing. The chaperones seemed to enjoy these as much as, if not more, thank the kids.

Most of the kids were here to have a good time, enjoy their last bash with friends, get pictures for the last time, get their yearbooks signed by friends, and get a bit looped on their three drinks or something else. Some kids went outside in groups of two or three to smoke, do a joint, make out, or hook up.

Tyler and his friends had a master plan they had been talking about for a month now. In addition to being the Class President, Kelly Reynolds was totally hot and known not to be dating anyone special. It was rumored that she had the hots for Tyler. They would find out tonight, for sure.

At ten, the DJ played a slow dance song, and Tyler approached Kelly, "How about a dance, Kelly?"

"Sure, Tyler," she said with a smile on her face as she stood and took his hand. "You haven't been with Debbie much tonight; what's that about?"

"You know, with college coming soon, we are cooling it and agreed that tonight would be a good time to play it single. I didn't see you with a date."

"No, just Barbara, Gloria, and me doing the girlfriend thing. I hear you finally committed to Duke next year."

"Yep, looking forward to it; how about you?"

"I'm staying close to home, MIT."

The song was ending, and *it was impossible for Kelly not to know I was attracted to her*, Tyler thought. *There are some things a guy cannot hide.*

"How about going outside for some fresh air and a beer? I've got two tickets left."

"Sure!"

They stopped by the bar and picked up two Samuel Adams, and Tyler led her outside. It was still mild outside, and on a clear night, the stars and half-moon were shining brightly. "Wow, what a gorgeous night," he said; *girls love that shit!*

They headed to the pool area, and Tyler knew the cabanas were unlocked. They could have some privacy there, at least for a bit. They entered and sat close to each other on a chaise lounge. Tyler raised his beer bottle and toasted, "To our futures, Kelly."

Kelly returned the toast, "To the Class of 2022!"

Tyler reached in and gave her a peck on the cheek. But he pulled back only an inch or two, waiting for her to glimpse into his eyes. When she did, he looked into hers and slowly inched closer to her lips. Her mouth opened invitingly, and he accepted the invitation. Their tongues found each other and explored. Tyler's arousal was now in full throttle, and it seemed that Kelly was keeping pace. Her hand found its way down to his zipper, but without opening it, she gently massaged it as it continued its growth. "Oh, Kelly, that feels so good; please don't stop."

She couldn't and wouldn't! She started unbuckling his belt as he reached around and began unzipping her dress. By the time he had worked it down to her waist, Kelly had slumped, and her body fell out of Tyler's arms, collapsing onto the chaise lounge.

Tyler froze for a minute, and then Nathan, Billy, and Sheldon entered the cabana.

"She's out cold," Tyler said. "Those roofies are quick-acting. Guys, I'm still hard; I'm going first."

Chapter 11

June 10, 2022, Emporia

The only similarity between the graduations at Greensville County High School and Beaver County Day School was the size of the graduating class: one hundred fifteen at Greensville. Of those one hundred fifteen, twenty-seven were Hispanic, five Caucasian, and the remaining eighty-seven were Black.

Their post-high school prospects were also limited; only eighteen were admitted to colleges; the rest would start working at the railroad, the local hotels and fast-food restaurants, light construction, or in retail as salesclerks.

Lincoln Anderson was, of course, granted a full basketball scholarship to Richmond Commonwealth University and was the toast of the town. Satchel Abney had made the trip over from Newport News for today's graduation. Len Goldstein decided to remain on Hilton Head and allow Satchel the spotlight. He deserved it.

Coach Blackwell of RCU also made the trip down from Richmond to congratulate his newest recruit. Blackwell sat with Satch Abney as, other than the Anderson family, and they only knew the other.

The graduation was held in the school auditorium, with a luncheon celebration afterward in the school's gymnasium. They had found Lincoln and his parents in the gym, and Dwight and Estelle Anderson dragged their family over to hug and thank Coach and Satchel. They introduced all their family members, and Estelle said, "We just do not know how to thank you both. This day is so much happier than it would have been because of your caring for Lincoln and our family. I wish Len Goldstein could be here, but he assured me he would collect a hug at Lincoln's first game in December."

Coach Blackwell said, "Satch here, and Len get the credit, Mrs. Anderson. I feel I am the beneficiary of their persistence. And it cost me a bundle as, out of guilt, I became a client of Len's firm. But I am not complaining; we are looking forward to having Lincoln at RCU. I hope you will all come up for Freshman Orientation Day next month."

"We would not miss it," added Dwight Anderson. "It is a very happy day for our family. Lincoln is the first in our family to go to college; I hope this will become a trend for the Andersons."

Speak for your own family, Dwight," Estelle said. "Some of my family up in Philly have been to college. Lincoln's cousin Claudia is a lawyer up in Philly."

Lincoln said, "And Bo Campbell, the best ballplayer in the family, will most likely be going to Villanova next year."

"Wait! Your cousin is Bo Campbell?" Blackwell asked. "The first report I received from Future Stars two weeks ago had Campbell listed as the number one high school prospect in next year's class. Any chance of a family reunion?"

"Nice try, coach, but you are really late to that dance. I think Jay Wright had the kid under contract before he could write his name," Dwight Anderson responded.

Satch Abney interrupted, "I'm going to let you people enjoy your day with your family; I've got a long ride back to Newport News. I'm very glad I could be here, and congratulations to all of you. I'll certainly come to see you play next season, Linc!"

Coach Blackwell said, "Hey, I'll walk out with you, Satch; I've overstayed my welcome; we'll talk soon, Linc, and see y'all next month. Congratulations again on your graduation, Lincoln."

More hugs and some more tears, and the Coach and Satch Abney departed. The Andersons resumed the party.

There was no Country Club party that night, even though several of the kids held small parties at their homes that included their parents and families. This included the Andersons. Alcohol was not provided to the kids.

There were no reports of alcohol, drugs, roofings, or rapes.

Chapter 12

June 25, 2022, Emporia

As he had done the last two years, Lincoln Anderson was working this summer at Wendy's, which was just off Exit 11 in Emporia. Even with a full scholarship, he knew he would need some of his own money for incidentals, eating out, movies, and even a date or two. His parents said they would help, but he enjoyed the work and met a couple of kids last summer who were also returning.

Summer was the busy season for all the retail shops along I-95 as vacationers traveled to the beaches of the Carolinas, Georgia, and Florida. Every exit offered fast food from McDonald's, Burger King, Wendy's, Hardee's, Arby's, and Pizza Hut, along with the same hotel chains and restaurants like Cracker Barrel. None of the teenagers who wanted to work had any trouble finding opportunities.

Lincoln preferred Wendy's as they served breakfast; thus, he could work a seven AM – four PM shift three or four days a week and not have to work at night. He was scheduled on Tuesdays, Thursdays, and Saturdays and would pick up a fourth day if someone needed off.

Two years ago, he walked the mile and a half to Wendy's; last year, he rode his bike. This year, his mom was letting him use her 2018 Hyundai Sonata on Saturday so he could go out with friends after work. Saturday, June 29th, was no different than any other summer day in Southern Virginia, hot and humid. When Lincoln got to work at six-fifty, it was already seventy-eight degrees. The cooks got there an hour earlier, and the place smelled of bacon, sausage, and hash browns. Lincoln gobbled down a breakfast sandwich, put on his shirt and hat, and was ready to go.

Lincoln was already looking forward to four o'clock, when his shift would end, as he had plans after work with Ron Dexter and Breanna White, two work friends. He had a bit of a crush on Breanna, and he thought it was mutual. He had a plan to drop Ron off first and have some private time with Breanna.

With many of the nearby hotels offering free breakfast, the morning was slow, but at eleven, the late breakfast and early lunch diners collided, and things picked up. Lincoln moved from the counter to the fries station, to the take-out window over his shift, with two half-hour breaks that he took outside. He thought about writing to Ms. Wendy to say that they needed some traffic control in the kitchen. He estimated that in an eight-hour shift, there were one hundred and fifty collisions, bump-intos, near spills, or get-out-of-my-ways.

But four o'clock eventually arrived, and he, Ron, and Brianna walked out to his car. Ron agreed to grant Lincoln's earlier request and sit in the back, allowing Brianna upfront.

"Where are we eating?" Lincoln asked.

That was easy! *FIVE GUYS, Burgers, and Fries* was the unanimous choice, and Lincoln headed there, about a mile from Wendy's on the other side of I-95. It was four-forty by the time they ordered, picked up, and topped their burgers. But they were in no hurry, as none of them had any other plans for Saturday night.

This was the first time the three of them had been anywhere together except for Wendy's, of course. Lincoln knew Ron and Brianna both were a year younger than him and had just finished their junior years.

Ron said to Lincoln, "Everyone in school was talking about your scholarship to RCU, Lincoln; how did that happen?"

"Do you believe in miracles? I had absolutely no plan to go to college, and with two weeks left in the season, a Black guy from Newport News and a Jewish guy from Philly cornered me and my parents after the game and then came to the house the next morning to talk. It turns out the white dude is a big-time talent evaluator and sells his ratings to colleges and the NBA teams. They tell me they can get me into college, blah, blah, and a week later, Coach Blackwell is at my game. Me and my parents talk with him and on the spot, he offers me a full scholarship. I am in shock, my mother is in tears, and my dad just keeps asking him more questions."

"That is so cool, Lincoln," Brianna chimes in. "I don't know a whole lot about basketball, but you must be really good."

"Funny thing, Bri, I always knew I was pretty good but never suspected I was THAT good until Mr. Goldstein, Goldy, I'm allowed to call him, told me how high he was going to rank me and that he guaranteed me I could play college ball. Coach Blackwell agreed with him."

Ron added, "Maybe we can go up to see a game, Bri; that would be totally cool."

"I'm certain I'll be able to get you tickets; my parents expect to come up to all of the home games. Do you all have any plans after high school?"

"I'm thinking about a graphic arts program at the community college in Stony Creek," Brianna said.

Ron added, "That's funny because I am also thinking of something in the tech field. I have written one game already, and I have several more in mind. But I'm not certain how to make a living doing it. So, I don't know about college; perhaps a tech school."

Bri said, "You should look in the community college; I'd bet they have a program for gamers."

"Good idea!"

They spent another hour getting to know each other, and at six-thirty, they cleaned up and left.

Chapter 13

Lincoln first drove Ron home. He lives on the Southwest end of town, out by the reservoir. Ron directed him to Sunset Lane, and he jumped out of the car, hollering, "Thanks for the ride, Lincoln; see you both next week."

They drove off. Brianna lived on the other side of the Interchange. She told Lincoln she was just off Carroll Street. When they got to Carroll, she said, "First street there on the right is Gay Street; that's me!"

"I never heard of Gay Street, and Emporia's not that big."

"It literally is a one-block street; when you drop me off, at the end of the street, turn left onto West End. I think you can take that all the way to your house or go back over to Carroll. West End is a bit desolate, and my parents tell me to avoid it, which I am glad to do. Here we are, 170."

Lincoln pulled over and said, "You work next Saturday?"

"I think so!"

"Would you want to go out afterward, just the two of us, and grab something to eat?"

"That would be cool; I'll have to ask my mom and dad, but I think they'll be fine. I'll let you know at work Thursday or text you."

"Great, I'll see you Thursday, Bri!"

"OK, and thanks for the ride home, Lincoln."

She jumped out of the car and went up the short walk, turned around, and waved again.

As he pulled away, Lincoln thought to himself, *that went well—a real date next Saturday night.*

At the end of her block, he hit West End, just as Bri said he would, and he turned left. Even though this section was quite abandoned and depressed, it was only four to five blocks from Main Street, where it ended. But Lincoln would not get that far.

Between Taylor and Greene Streets, he saw a bike lying on the road. *A strange place for an abandoned bike*, he thought. It was a narrow, one-way street, so Lincoln had to pull off onto the grass. He parked and got out. He walked towards the bike, and as he got within ten feet, he noticed a young girl lying in the drainage ditch. He ran over to her, knelt down, and gently pushed her to see if she was awake. There was no movement.

He ran back to his car and dialed 9-1-1 on his cell phone.

"This is 9-1-1; what is your emergency?"

"Yes, I am on West End, and a girl has fallen off her bike, and she's not moving. I think she needs an ambulance really bad."

"Where on West End?"

"Right at Taylor and Greene."

"And your name, sir?"

"Lincoln Anderson."

"OK, Mr. Anderson, please wait for the ambulance and police, and do not touch the girl. They should be there within five minutes."

She hung up. Lincoln thought he should call home; hopefully, his dad could come over. He dialed his dad's cell.

"What's up, Lincoln?"

"Hi, dad, can you get over to West End? I was driving home and saw a bike lying on the ground. When I went over to it, there was a girl lying in the ditch next to it. I called 9-1-1, and they are on their way, but I hope you can get here."

"I'll be right there, Lincoln. You did the right thing, but do not answer any questions until I get there. Do you hear me? Is there anyone else there? Other drivers pulled over?"

"Not yet!"

"I'm on my way."

Ten minutes later, a police car arrived, and Lincoln could hear the ambulance approaching behind them. Lincoln got out of the car and walked towards the girl. Two uniformed police officers jumped out of their car; one pulled his gun and said, "Halt right there, young man; put your hands up in the air?"

The other officer walked to the girl's body and placed his hand on her throat. He turned and said, "She's gone."

They both walked towards Lincoln and said, "Keep your hands in the air. We just need to search you; do you have a weapon?"

"No, I don't have any weapon; what am I a suspect? I just saw the girl's bike and stopped to see if I could help."

The officer frisked Lincoln and then looked into his pockets. Out of his side pocket, he pulled out a small pouch that contained a white powdery substance. "What's this?"

"What do you mean? That's not mine, whatever it is."

"Turn around, smart Alec. We are taking you into the station for questioning; turn around; cuff him, Buddy."

"Wait, what the hell is this? I ain't done nothing."

The officer grabbed Lincoln and forcibly turned him around. Lincoln stumbled, falling to the ground. One officer kicked him in the butt, while the other pulled out a club and hit him several times on the shoulder. "Now, are you going to get in the car peacefully, or do we need more discipline?"

Just then, Lincoln's father pulled up and jumped out of his car, "What's going on here? Why is my son on the ground?"

"Who are you?"

"I'm Lincoln's father, Dwight Anderson; who are you?"

"I am Officer Jerome Abbott, and this is Officer Buddy Wilkins with the Emporia Police Department. Your son stumbled when we were putting the handcuffs on him. We are taking your son in for questioning about this young woman's death and this substance we found on him," showing the white pouch to Anderson.

"Dad, whatever that is, it ain't mine. This guy just reached into my pocket and pulled it out like it was a magic trick. And they have been kicking and clubbing me."

"Is this the way you treat all your suspects or only the Black kids? Lincoln let's just go down the station and get this sorted out. Don't say a word. Officers, I'll follow you, but do not ask my son any questions until I arrive."

The ambulance had removed the girl's body after a forensics team had examined and taken pictures. They got into their respective cars and made off for the police station. Dwight Anderson placed a call to his wife, explained the situation to her, and asked her to remain calm and call Malcolm Grimsley, their friend and attorney.

Chapter 14

June 10, The Country Club, Brookline

At eleven-ten that night, one of the students whispered to a server, "There seems to be a young lady passed out in one of the cabanas," and she kept walking.

This was not a terribly unusual occurrence at these types of parties, but Yvonne Hicks still felt the need to advise the Catering Manager, Arthur Bowden. Bowden summoned the security chief, "Lester, let's go out to the cabanas; we have a report of a young woman passed out."

They walked out together and, in the third cabana, found one of the graduates passed out on the chaise lounge. Fleming checked on the young woman and immediately jumped on his cell phone, "This is Lester Fleming at The Country Club. I have a young woman here who is passed out and has a very weak pulse. I need an ambulance on the QT, and please notify the local police. This is urgent, please."

"Are the police necessary, Les?" Bowden asked.

"Afraid so, Art. It's not likely that this young lady came out here alone and drank herself to near death. There is no alcohol in the cabana. If this goes bad, we'd have hell to pay for not calling the police tonight. Let's hope it turns out to be nothing."

"I'm sure you are right. Will you remain here while I track down one of the chaperones or school officials? I don't see a handbag, and we need to identify the girl ASAP."

Ten minutes later, Art Bowden returned with Colleen Lassiter, Beaver's Dean of Students. The EMTs had the young woman on the stretcher and were rolling it toward the ambulance when Bowden called, "Hold on, please. We would like Ms. Lassiter here to try and identify the young woman."

They stopped, and Ms. Lassiter walked up to the stretcher, "Oh my, that is Kelly Reynolds, the Class President; what can I tell her parents?"

Lester Fleming, the security guard, had joined the group, and the EMTs and Bowden looked at him, neither wanting to be the one to answer that question. Fleming responded, "Right now, I would suggest saying that it appears she had too much to drink and was found passed out. They are taking her to the Beth Israel Medical Center. At this point, that's not too much of a stretch; I am sure the doctors will know by the time they get to the hospital."

The party was over, but the four uniformed police officers and two detectives had locked down the facility, and no one was to leave, including the Country Club employees. Detective Richard Duffy was fifty-five years old, a bit overweight, and balding. He grew up in Quincy, ten miles south of Boston. After four years as a Military Policeman in the Marines, he decided law enforcement was his calling. He joined the Boston Police Department, where he met his wife, Cindy. After passing his detective exam in 2005, they moved to Needham, and he joined the Brookline Police Department.

Duffy assumed command, and once everyone was settled in the ballroom, he took the DJ's microphone. "Please quiet down! I am Detective Richard Duffy of the Brookline Police, and my partner, Kathy Flanagan, is over there," pointing towards Kathy. "One of your classmates, Kelly Reynolds, was found passed out in one of the cabanas and has been taken to the nearest hospital. Due to the hour of the night, we will not hold extensive interviews tonight; we do want to get all of your names and ask when you may have last seen Miss Reynolds. I would suggest calling your parents and letting them know that you may be delayed. Tell them not to come here as they will not be admitted to the facility. If they plan to pick you up, tell them you will call them after you are released.

"We have six of us here, so we should be able to get through this in about an hour. We appreciate your cooperation and patience."

The police officers and detectives had set up interview stations off the lobby, and the chaperones, after being interviewed themselves, would retrieve students as the interviewers were ready for them.

Detective Duffy started with Yvonne Hicks; the other officers started with the chaperones, faculty, and Club Management. Duffy said to Hicks, "I understand you found the young woman?

"No, not exactly. One of the students told me they had seen her sleeping in the cabana, so I told my Supervisor, Mr. Bowden. He and the security guard went out to the cabana. So, I never saw the girl."

"What can you tell me about the girl who told you about Miss Reynolds?"

"I am embarrassed to say, but almost nothing. I'm not even certain I looked up. I think she was wearing a black cocktail type of dress and had blondish hair, but that's it, I'm afraid."

"Anything else? Was her hair up, any tattoos, birthmarks, the color of her shoes, anything at all?"

"I'm sorry, but no. It just seemed such a routine thing; her voice did not seem panicked at all, just 'someone is asleep in one of the cabanas.' It seemed she was just afraid we would leave her there all night."

"Have you looked around? Do you recognize anyone?"

"Afraid not, they all look the same to me; black dresses were quite popular tonight."

"OK, Ms. Hicks, we may need to speak with you again, but that's all for now. Thank you."

This went on for about an hour, and once everyone had been interviewed and released, Duffy gathered the officers, security guards, Art Bowden, and Colleen Lassiter at a large table in the ballroom.

"Let's debrief and see what we have. The server who got the first message cannot recall anything about the girl who gave it to her, only that she had a black dress on. Several kids mentioned seeing Kelly and said she did not seem to be drunk. Two girls mentioned seeing her dance with Tyler Longenecker. They remembered this because Tyler was a well-known jock and thought to be dating Debbie Gibson. Can anyone add to that? Did anyone interview this Tyler kid or his girlfriend?"

For the next twenty minutes, they compared their stories and raised questions and hypotheticals. Duffy thought he should summarize, "OK, I think this is what we've got. A good number of the kids recall Longenecker and Reynolds dancing, and four kids mentioned them walking outside somewhere between nine-forty-five and ten-fifteen. No one recalls seeing either of them after that. Longenecker nor his girlfriend, Debbie Gibson, were still here to be interviewed. Perhaps they left together sometime after ten-thirty. Tomorrow, Ms. Lassiter will reconcile the two lists, those interviewed tonight against the total attendee list, and that will let us know who remains to be interviewed.

"Perhaps by then, we'll have good news about Kelly Reynolds and at least a preliminary report on what might have happened to her. We should also know what evidence or DNA may have been collected in the cabana and if the young girl may have had sex that night. Did I miss anything?"

They all looked at their notes, then at each other, shrugging in the negative.

"Nothing? OK, I'll need your notes, but make certain Ms. Lassiter has a list of those you interviewed. Lastly, I know y'all didn't sign up for this, and I sincerely appreciate all your assistance and diligence. I think we did the best we could do, given the circumstances. The party is over; good night and thank you again."

They stood, talked a bit, gave Lassiter their lists and Duffy their notes, and said their goodbyes.

The party may have been over, but the investigation was just getting started.

Chapter 15

Beth Israel Medical Center, Brookline

Detective Duffy and his partner, Kathy Flanagan, arrived at the Beth Israel Medical Center at twelve-twenty AM and went to the ER. The woman at reception told them that Kelly Reynolds was in a coma and was being attended to by a medical team. She nodded towards a far corner of the Waiting Room and identified Reynolds' parents, sitting with Colleen Lassiter from the Beaver School and another unidentified man. They thanked her and walked towards the group.

The Emergency Room at Beth Israel was modern and well-furnished, clearly trying to make families and friends as comfortable as possible during their often anxiety-filled wait. There was an electronic board showing those currently being treated or waiting to be treated and which bay or OR they were in.

The furniture was comfortable and spaced out to allow for private conversations between family members or the hospital staff. There were several vending machines for nourishment and a complimentary Keurig machine to help keep those sitting vigil awake.

"Mr. and Mrs. Reynolds?" Duffy inquired.

"Yes?" Richard Reynolds responded.

"I am Detective Duffy, and this is my partner, Detective Flanagan. How is your daughter doing?"

"She is in a coma, and the doctors are running tests to determine if they need to do surgery. We hope to see a doctor soon."

At that point, Colleen Lassiter said, "Detectives, this is Dr. Breckenridge, our Headmaster."

They shook hands, "Good to meet you, even though I wish it were not under such circumstances," Dr. Breckenridge said. "Can you tell us anymore?"

Duffy replied, "Not really; Ms. Lassiter knows what we know. We interviewed eighty-four of the one hundred and sixteen students and dates who attended. Thirty-two had already left, including a couple that are on the top of our list to speak with."

Turning to the Reynolds, Duffy asked, "Did your daughter have a date at the party?"

Elizabeth Reynolds replied, "No, she did not have a serious boyfriend, so she decided to go with a couple of girlfriends."

"Kelly was a pretty, intelligent, and popular young woman; are you aware of any jealousies or rejected suitors?"

"Not that I am aware of, but even though I think my daughter and I are very close, I'm not certain she would make me aware of those unless they had become quite serious."

"Dr. Breckenridge and Miss Lassiter, can you tell us a bit about the drug culture at school?"

Lassiter looked at her boss, clearly preferring he take that question; finally, he did, "It is not something we are unconcerned about, Detective. These young people are affluent and, therefore, have money to explore that world. Of course, most of it goes on outside of the school premises, but our staff can often see the symptoms. A year ago, we had a junior die of an overdose of oxycodone, and in the last two years, we have had three reports of young women being roofied. Only one of the boys was identified, and he was expelled and reported to the police."

"Roofied?" Mrs. Reynolds asked"

Kelly Flanagan replied to that, "Roofied refers to being given Rohypnol, the date rape drug."

"Oh, great!"

Just then, a middle-aged man in surgical green scrubs approached them, "Mr. and Mrs. Reynolds?"

"That's us, yes," Mrs. Reynolds responded for both of them.

"I'm Dr. Roberts; I have been attending to Kelly. Might I have a minute, please?"

"Certainly, but you may speak in front of these people; these are the detectives and our daughter's school officials. They'll want to hear the update."

"Very well! As you know, Kelly is in a coma that appears to have been induced by the combination of alcohol and Rohypnol. We are going to keep her in a coma and allow the antibiotics to go to work. We are keeping the pressure off her brain to minimize any damage, and right now, we are optimistic there hasn't been any. We would expect to keep her in this coma for 24-48 hours, so we do not expect to have much more to tell you for a while.

"I must ask you if you know if your daughter has been sexually active?"

Again, Mrs. Reynolds took that question, "I know that she is not a virgin, but I also know she is not promiscuous. I know that she's had sex with two boys, but none that I am aware of in the last year. Why?"

"She had sex last night, either consensual or rape, after the Rohypnol took effect. A condom was used, so we did not recover any semen for DNA testing."

"Shit! I'll kill the bastard who did this," Mr. Reynolds exclaimed.

Mrs. Reynolds asked, "Is it too soon to predict her recovery, doctor?"

"Always the first question I get, Mrs. Reynolds, and you know I cannot guarantee anything just yet. But I can tell you that we are quite fortunate that she got treatment as quickly as she did. We were told that the best guess was that she may have ingested the drug at about ten-thirty, and we had her here by eleven-forty-five. There is a noticeable difference in recoveries when that period is three to four hours. The unknown is still the drug dosage and the alcohol mix. But I am optimistic that we got to her in time, and right now, she seems strong, and her vitals are stable."

Detective Duffy asked, "Can you predict just how much she might recall when she awakens?"

"That's impossible to predict. She may not even recall going to the party, or what boys she may have danced with, or how much alcohol she drank. She will most likely not recall when the drug was administered or who did that, and certainly nothing about the rape, if that is what it was."

"Thanks, doctor; we'll discuss if we are both staying or whatever. Who will be our contact when you leave?"

"The staff here in the ER will always know the status and the attending physician. If you both decide to go home, we will call should there be any change in her condition. I have two other surgeries in the morning, but I'll check in on her tomorrow afternoon. Please continue to remain positive, and good luck."

The doctor walked off, leaving the six of them standing there in silence, all a bit stunned by what they had just heard.

Duffy said, "I hope the next time we see you all is when we are bedside talking to your smiling daughter. The next day or two, we will be focused on interviewing the rest of the students and perhaps re-interviewing a couple of them. We'll be in touch, and here is my card should you need me. Good luck! It sounds like they got her here in time, and all will turn out for the best."

They all shook hands, promised to be in touch, and went their separate ways, leaving Mr. and Mrs. Reynolds in the ER.

Chapter 16

June 25th, Emporia

Officers Abbott and Wilkins had deposited Lincoln in the interview room and decided to let him simmer a bit as they went to the breakroom for some coffee. They noticed the kid's father enter the station but ignored him; let the desk clerk manage him for now.

Fifteen minutes later, they walked out to the lobby to get Lincoln's father, who was now speaking to another Black man. "Mr. Anderson, we are going to interview your son now; you may join us."

He got up and said, "This is our attorney, Mr. Grimsley; he'll be joining us."

"I would like a few minutes with my client before any interview; has he been charged with anything?"

"No! We just want to chat with him about the death of the young girl he claims to have found dead on the side of the road. You've got ten minutes," showing them into the room where Lincoln sat. Grimsley closed the door behind them and looked around for monitors or microphones, not seeing any.

"Hi, Lincoln; I am Malcolm Grimsley, an attorney and friend of your dad's. Assume this room is bugged but tell me what you can about what went down out there."

"I can't believe this shit is happening; this is a short story. I dropped off a girl I work with out on Gay Street in the Southwest. I was on my way home on West End Boulevard, and I saw a bike lying next to the road. I got out to see if anyone was there, and I saw this white girl lying in the drainage ditch. I go back to my car and call 9-1-1, and these two dudes show up and roughed me up, claiming they found some drugs on me. It's bullshit, I swear."

"Did you touch the girl?"

"I think I did; I just sort of rolled her over to see if she was awake or conscious."

"Did you recognize the girl?"

"No, sir!"

"And what have you told the police?"

"Just what I told you."

"Dwight, this is bullshit! I want to arrange a Press Conference when we are done here. They are trying to railroad this young Black kid for no other reason than he's Black. We've had too much of that in this town."

"Maybe they'll just let him go after we talk here."

"Possibly, but I want to be ready."

Grimsley takes out his cell phone, "Gloria, Mr. G here; sorry to call you at home, but can you call and make arrangements for a press conference tomorrow morning, nine o'clock, at the police station? I know it's Sunday, but a good story doesn't wait for working hours. Make certain you call Diane Witherspoon at WKTR and that she has cameras there."

"Sure, can I tell them the subject?"

"Yeah, a young Black kid getting roughed up and framed for a crime he did not commit? Unusual, right?"

"Got it, Mr. G; I'll text you in a bit."

Grimsley opened the door and waved Abbott and Wilkins in.

Abbott said, "We are not recording this, and we have not yet charged Mr. Anderson here with a crime. Can you tell us how and why you happened to come across this young girl?"

Lincoln wasn't certain if he should reply, so he looked to Grimsley, who nodded his approval to answer. "As I told you before, I was just driving home on West End Boulevard and saw the bike lying on the road. I pulled over and got out of the car. Then I saw her lying in the ditch. I went over to her and pulled her towards me so I could see if she was awake or sleeping. When she didn't move, I got back into my car and called 9-1-1. Then y'all arrived, and the shitshow started."

"You are sure you did not hit this girl and knock her off her bike?"

"Absolutely not!"

"And the drugs?"

"I know nothing about any drugs, not mine. You planted them."

"Watch that, son; you accusing me of planting evidence on you?"

Grimsley chimed in, "Officer, my client has very clearly said that the drugs were not his and that he has never done drugs, and yet you persist on this accusation. If it was not planted, you figure out an explanation."

"Do you know the girl?"

"No, sir!"

"Did you see any other cars or pedestrians in the area?"

"No, sir!"

"So, your story is that you just stumbled on this dead girl called 9-1-1, and the drugs are not yours?"

"That's not my story, sir; those are the facts."

"Your version of the facts!"

"Are we done here, officers?" Grimsley interceded.

"Yes! We are not going to arrest or charge you tonight, but you are not to leave town. We will most likely want to talk to you again on Monday."

On the steps of the Emporia Police Headquarters, Malcolm Grimsley, Dwight Anderson, and his son, Lincoln, paused to discuss the next step.

"I want to have this Press Conference in the morning. I believe it is important that we get in front of this narrative rather than have the police arrest you, and we are on the defensive."

"But will this affect my future at RCU? I can't imagine the coach will be happy to hear about this."

"Lincoln, it will be worse if we don't get your innocence out sooner rather than later. Sure, you'll hear from the coach, but if we get this dismissed within the next week or so, all will be good; trust me on this."

"Dad?"

"I agree with you both; so much for being a Good Samaritan. I wonder how many cars might have driven by that bike, not wanting to get involved? I'm proud of you, Lincoln. I'm wondering if we should contact Lenny Goldstein. He's the fellow who introduced us to Coach Blackwell at RCU. He might want to contact Blackwell or have some advice. And I am thinking of asking my wife to call her uncle up in Philly. He collaborated with a Black cop up there to hunt down the guy who murdered his father."

Grimsley replied, "I think having a Black cop down here could be helpful; it will keep these guys on their toes. He'll have no jurisdiction, of course, but his presence could make a real statement that we don't trust the locals. I'd like you both here tomorrow morning by 8:30; we good?"

"We're good, Mal; see you in the morning."

"Thank you, Mr. Grimsley," Lincoln added.

"Try not to worry about this, Lincoln; I still want to believe that the truth wins in the end," Grimsley said.

Lincoln and his dad got home to an anxious family, and they had to regurgitate it all, from the stop and arrest to the meeting on the steps with Malcolm Grimsley.

After hearing all the details, Estelle Anderson said, "I hope I did not overstep, but I called my Uncle James up in Philly."

Dwight and Lincoln looked at each other with smiles.

"Whatcha y'all smiling about?"

"We were going to ask you to do that in the morning. You beat us to it; what did he say?"

"He said he was going to talk to Detective Brown, and either he or both of them would be down here no later than Monday."

Lincoln's sister Tawana had been sitting in and could no longer hold it in, "So, how was your date Linc?"

Estelle Anderson replied for her son, "You know Tawana, which is like asking Mrs. Lincoln how she enjoyed the show."

It was time to sit down and have the Chinese food that was delivered an hour ago. They tried to lighten the conversation as they all chowed down on Moo Shu pork and egg rolls.

Chapter 17

June 26th, Emporia Police Station

Even at eight-thirty in the morning, it was a hot one: eighty degrees going to ninety, and the humidity was a sticky eighty-five. There were some dark clouds in the Southwest, and no one would be shocked by a thunderstorm.

Grimsley was not expecting a huge turnout from the media; after all, this was Emporia, Virginia, not New York, or even Richmond, for that matter. But Grimsley was pleased to see Diane Witherspoon and her mobile unit from WKTR TV. Several of the local Black Ministers had agreed to move their nine o'clock service to ten so their parishioners could attend in support.

The rest of the local and regional media would pick up the story from social media.

It was business as usual at the police station; they tried to ignore the activity, but they'd be paying attention to every word. Grimsley was certain of it.

Promptly at nine, Grimsley took to the microphone; *"Thank you all for being here on this glorious Sunday morning in Emporia. Standing with me today are Lincoln Anderson and his family. You may know Lincoln from his basketball playing here at Greensville High and his scholarship to Richmond Commonwealth University.*

But we are not here today because of Lincoln's basketball success, but to tell y'all what has been going on in our streets and behind the walls of this police station. Yesterday afternoon, Lincoln was returning home from having a burger with two friends after their shift at Wendy's. After dropping the second friend off, he was heading home on West End Boulevard when he noticed a fallen bicycle off to the side of the road. Being the kind of kid Lincoln is, he stopped to see if anyone had fallen and needed assistance. He at once saw a girl in the drainage ditch who was not moving.

She was later identified as Vicky Hennessy of Emporia, and I am sad to tell you she was dead at the scene.

Lincoln returned to his car and called 9-1-1. Ten minutes later, two white police officers arrived, put handcuffs on Lincoln, threw him to the ground, beat him, and planted drugs on him. They then took him to the police station, where they interviewed him with me and his father present. They let him go with the demand that he does not leave Emporia.

Friends and Emporians, we have seen too many of these police intimidating, beating, and falsely accusing innocent Black men of various crimes. I need not remind you of just last year, Drew Lester being beaten to near death for presumably shoplifting.

This is a national epidemic brought home right here to Emporia, and we are here to say that we have had it, Black Lives Matter, and we will shout it from the rooftops until we get the attention, respect, and fair treatment we deserve.

Thank you, my brothers and sisters, and please keep the Hennessy family in our prayers.

The hundred or so in attendance started cheering and chanting, "Black Lives Matter, Black Lives Matter."

Malcolm Grimsley had certainly stirred the pot; would it simmer or boil over?

Up in Philadelphia, James McNeil called his good friend and police detective, Vernon Brown, "Hey James, what gives on a Sunday morning?"

"Didn't wake you, did I, Vern?"

"Nah, what's up?"

"You feel like a road trip to Emporia, Virginia?"

"There's a story, no doubt."

James gave Vernon the story. Vernon told him that if he could clear it with his captain and his wife, not in that order, he'd be glad to do it.

By two o'clock, they were in the car, heading South.

Chapter 18

June 12th, Brookline

Detectives Duffy and Flanagan had decided the interviews could wait until Monday morning. That might allow Kelly Reynolds' status to improve, hopefully. If she recovered, the boys involved would be guilty of drug and rape charges; if she dies, they will add negligent homicide.

But nothing had changed by Monday morning, and after the eight o'clock meeting at the station, they took off for the Longenecker home.

It was a beautiful early summer day in New England, not a cloud in the sky and a comfortable seventy-five degrees. Duffy was doing the driving, and they knew they were heading to a ritzy neighborhood out near the Brookline Reservoir. They had Googled the Longeneckers and learned he was a partner in a prestigious law firm in the city.

They pulled into a circular driveway with three late-model cars; Duffy wondered how many more might be in the four-car garage. The landscaping and garden were all professionally maintained. Early summer flowers were in bloom. It was hard not to be impressed.

Duffy knocked at the door, which was promptly answered by a young Black woman who appeared to be housecleaning. "May I help you," she politely asked.

Removing their badges, Duffy said, "I'm sure! We are Detectives Duffy and Flanagan to see Tyler, please."

"May I tell him what this is in reference to?"

"Yes, the graduation party Saturday night at The Country Club."

She allowed them to step in and have a seat in the well-appointed foyer. They could not see much from the foyer except for what appeared to be a sitting room off to the side of the foyer. Even that was lavishly furnished.

After several minutes, a tall, good-looking fifty-ish man approached them and said, "Good morning, officers. I am Everett Longenecker, Tyler's father. May I ask what this is regarding?"

"Certainly; there was an incident at the graduation party Saturday night, and we are interviewing all the students who were there. It seemed that Tyler and others had left before we arrived."

"What type of incident?"

"Is that important? I'm certain Tyler knows about it by now if you don't."

"I'll call him down; please be seated in the sitting room," pointing to the room off the foyer.

Duffy and Flanagan chose seats next to each other on a plush loveseat. Two minutes later, father and son appeared, choosing armchairs after the introductions and handshakes.

"May I offer you coffee?"

Duffy and Flanagan had agreed that Duffy would do the questioning, and Flanagan could ask anything he may have omitted before they finished. She would also take notes.

"No, thank you," Duffy replied for both of them; "This should not take long. Tyler, do you know about Kelly Reynolds?"

"Yes, I saw on Instagram that she was in a coma; how is she?"

"Still in a coma. We are asking everyone at the party what they might have seen. Can you tell us, Tyler, what time you arrived at The Country Club and with whom?"

Tyler nervously looked at his father as if waiting for his approval to answer. None was forthcoming.

"It was a bit before eight; the party started at seven-thirty, and Debbie Gibson's parents wanted to take a few pictures at her house when I picked her up."

"And for the record, who is Debbie Gibson?"

"Debbie has been my girlfriend for the last year and a half; she also graduated."

"And did you see Kelly Reynolds at the party?"

"Sure! As Class President, this was the Kelly Show; she greeted everyone and was center stage all night."

"Do you know her very well, and did you speak with her that night?"

"Everyone knows Kelly, detective, but I cannot say I knew her very well. We ran in different circles, but she was in a couple of my classes, so we would occasionally chat. And we had one dance at the party, so we obviously spoke then."

"So, you did not dance exclusively with your girlfriend? I'm not up on that stuff these days."

"Debbie and I agreed we would pretty much hang with our own friends at the party. We are going to separate colleges in the Fall, and we were going to cool our relationship over the summer. Debbie was cool with that."

"Several students told us that they saw you and Kelly go outside; do you recall what time that was?"

"I wasn't paying much attention to time, but if I had to guess, I'd say it was between nine-thirty and ten."

"And then?"

"What? I wanted to go back in, and she wanted to stay out a bit longer. So, I did. I did not see her again the rest of the night."

"What time did you leave?"

"I would have to say it was close to ten-thirty. I left with Nate Friedlander, Billy Bender, and Shelly Warner. Billy didn't drink, so he drove my car. We all stayed at Billy's, and I called home to let them know where I was; do you recall the time, Dad?"

"I would say it was about eleven-thirty."

Sensing they were close to ending, Kathy Flanagan asked, "Did you notice any drugs or alcohol, other than the wine and beer being served?"

"I had a pint of vodka with me, and some other kids also had some tequila and bourbon. I noticed the smell of weed when Kelly and I stepped outside. But that was it."

"Was Debbie Gibson OK with your leaving without her? I mean, you brought her to the party," Flanagan asked.

"I, of course, asked her, and she said she'd get a ride with a girlfriend or call her parents. She said it was no problem."

"Anything else we should know?"

"I don't think so; I sure hope Kelly is OK."

Duffy and Flanagan looked at each other and stood. Duffy thanked them both and said he'd call if there were any further questions.

When they got to the car, Duffy asked, "What do you think, Kath?"

"He had his answers well-rehearsed, but the timeline is tight. It seems that he and Kelly dancing, going outside, his returning inside, Kelly's drugging and rape, and her discovery all happened between ten and eleven. Possible, I guess!"

"But if we put fifteen minutes on each end for those estimates, which would be an hour and a half, a more practical timeline."

"Debbie Gibson's next, boss?"

"Let's do it! Check the list to see who is scheduled to interview Tyler's friends; you got the names?"

"Yep!"

Chapter 19

Fifteen minutes later, they pulled into Gibson's driveway. While there was not as much real estate between the homes as in the Longenecker neighborhood, the homes looked every bit as lavish. No housekeeper answered the door; Mrs. Gibson herself opened it and introduced herself.

"Please come in, detectives; it's a terrible thing about Kelly. Is she going to be ok?"

This time, Kathy Flanagan would lead, thinking that a woman might make Gibson a bit more comfortable. "We just do not have an update as yet, Mrs. Gibson; is Debbie available?"

She's upstairs; I'll get her. May I bring you anything, coffee, water?"

"If not inconvenient, black coffee would be great," Duffy said.

"Make that two, thank you, "Kathy added.

Mrs. Gibson left to retrieve her daughter and coffee. Duffy and Flanagan looked around the very expensively furnished living room decorated with Asian carpets and pottery to go with the dark Ethan Allen furniture.

Mrs. Gibson returned with Debbie, made the introductions, and left to fetch coffee. Debbie sat down in a wing chair facing the sofa where the detectives sat, with the coffee table in between. To break the ice, Flanagan said, "Congratulations on your graduation, Debbie; you off to college?"

"Thank you, yes, I am starting Yale in the Fall!"

Mrs. Gibson entered with the coffee, and she tried to place it down without interrupting the conversation. Duffy and Flanagan thanked her, and Kathy continued.

"Is your husband at home, Mrs. Gibson?"

"Please call me Rhonda, and no, he's at work. Would you rather come back when he is here?"

"No, that's fine; if we need to speak with him, we'll call. I guess you know that we are interviewing all the students who were at the party on Saturday night. You apparently had left before we arrived."

"I'm not certain what time you arrived, but I left shortly after eleven with Cindy Moore; her mother picked us up."

"But you came to the party with Tyler Longenecker, as we understand it."

"Yes, but Tyler and I did not hang together at the party, and when he said he wanted to leave with Billy, Nate, and Shelly, I told him fine."

"So, you did not expect your boyfriend, who brought you to the party, to take you home?"

"Tyler is going to Duke in the Fall, and we mutually agreed to cool it for the summer. Plus, he was drinking quite heavily, and I'm not anxious to be around him when he's been drinking. So, I was delighted not to go home with him."

"During the Party, did you happen to notice whom Kelly Reynolds was hanging with?"

"Kelly was hanging with everyone. She doesn't have a steady guy but is liked by everyone, so she just made certain she saw and hugged everyone, including me. I did notice her dancing with Tyler, I must admit I was surprised at that."

"Surprised or jealous?"

"Surprised is the right word. I didn't even know that Tyler knew Kelly, and he never mentioned her. But Kelly is very attractive, and perhaps Tyler was looking for a summer replacement."

"You're a lot nicer than I would be, Debbie. Does Tyler fool around with any drugs?"

"Mom, you want to hear this?"

"I wouldn't miss it; please go on, Deb."

"First, let me tell you that I have done weed; I'm not crazy about it, but if I'm somewhere and they are passing it around, I might take a hit. And I once tried Oxy; that's it! I have not tried anything else. Tyler is much more adventurous and will try anything that does not involve a needle. So yes, I know he has tried Oxy, fentanyl, and I'm sure, some other stuff. But I honestly do not believe he's an addict; I think he just sees himself as a party boy. It's one of the reasons I was not jealous of his dancing with Kelly; Tyler and I were never going live happily ever after. At times, I didn't even like the guy."

"Last question from me, Debbie, do you believe that Tyler fooled around with other girls if you know what I mean?"

"I am not aware of it, but it wouldn't shock me; I think it fits that image he sees of himself."

"Anything else, Duff?"

"Just one, Debbie, if there was one boy at the party that might have done this to Kelly Reynolds, could you venture a guess who that might be?"

"I'm not sure what you mean, detective; did what? I just thought Kelly passed out drunk."

"We can't say more, but no, she did not just pass out."

"I just don't know who might have done that; I'm sorry!"

Chapter 20

June 27th, Emporia

James McNeil and Vernon Brown arrived in Emporia at seven-fifteen PM and checked in at the Marriott Courtyard. James had reserved two rooms; he and Vernon were close but not *that* close.

He called his niece, "Hello, Estelle, Vernon here; we just got into the hotel; anything new?"

"I told you about the news conference this morning. The local churches have organized a Non-Sectarian vigil at nine tonight at the site where the Hennessey girl was found. Blacks and Whites are expected; I'm not certain if we should go or not."

"I'd check with your attorney; I think he would suggest Lincoln not attend, but it might be nice if you do; ask him. I do not think we'll join you, but we will be over at eight in the morning. See you then, Estelle."

"Thanks so much for being here, Uncle James; see you in the morning; don't eat!"

Dwight and Estelle Anderson had decided to attend the vigil after receiving the blessing of Malcolm Grimsley. Cars were parked on West End Boulevard, in front of and behind the spot where Vicky Hennessey had been discovered. A makeshift memorial of candles and flowers marked the spot. About seventy-five people were there, many holding candles. It was a mixed crowd of white and black, young and old.

It certainly was not a cool night, but with the sundown and moderate humidity, the seventy-eight degrees was tolerable. Some dark clouds added to the possibility of a thundershower; many had brought umbrellas. Two squad cars and four officers were present, hoping their only role was traffic control.

Dwight and Estelle recognized their Pastor, Reverend Moore, standing in the front, but there was also a white clergyman with, they assumed, Vicky Hennessey's family.

"Good evening, friends! I am Father Sullivan of the Sacred Catholic Church of Emporia, and with me are the Hennessey Family and Reverend Ezekiel Gibson of the First Baptist Church of Greensville County. On behalf of the Hennessey family and Reverend Gibson, I wish to thank you for being here tonight to share in the grief of the Hennessey family and to remember and honor Vicky. It is our hope that we can come together as a community to help the Hennessey family deal with this horrific accident."

Vicky's parents chose not to speak, but several school friends sobbingly talked about how much she would be missed and what a funny and kind person she was.

The Reverend Moore led a prayer, and a dozen family members and friends offered tributes. When they seemed to be over, someone shouted, "So where is the Black kid that killed her?"

"Yeah, where is he?"

"This ain't the end of this shit!"

Father Sullivan exhorted, "Please; we will have none of that talk here. We have no idea who, if anyone, might be responsible for Vicky's death. We need to remain calm and let the police do their work. Our focus and prayers need to be with the Hennesseys."

Then, a Black member of the crowd yelled, "Then why are those police blaming a Black boy for it? Black Lives Matter! We cannot have our brother falsely accused."

Reverend Gibson responded, "Father Sullivan's admonishment applies to us all. We will certainly see that the Hennessey family gets answers and that all are treated fairly, white, or Black."

With that, the crowd began to disburse; the police had called for two more officers in case this shouting would erupt into something worse, but it appeared all were going quietly.

Not knowing anything about the Hennesseys, Dwight and Estelle Anderson thought it was best not to approach them, but they did briefly speak with Reverend Gibson.

Chapter 21

June 28th, Emporia

James and Vernon arrived promptly at eight o'clock Monday morning and parked in front of the Anderson home.

James McNeil knew what the Anderson family was going through. Just this past February, his grandson, Bo Campbell, had been falsely accused of murdering his best friend based on planted evidence. The charges were dropped when James and Vernon helped identify the actual killer as Reggie McIntosh, the Assistant Basketball Coach at Overbrook High School and part-time drug dealer.

Dwight Anderson stood out on his front stoop, awaiting their arrival. As they were getting out of the car, he walked down to greet them, extending his hand first to Vernon Brown; "Good morning, detective, thank you for being here. I'm Dwight Anderson, and I married into this McNeil family."

"I'm off duty, Dwight, so Vernon is fine. Good to be here; I hope we can help."

James had joined them by then carrying a large, unwrapped box and giving Dwight a man hug. "Good to see you, Dwight; how's the family holding up?"

"I guess OK; you've been through this shit. You hope it will turn out OK, but in this country, you can never be quite certain, can you?"

"You got that right, and I hope we can help. I can smell Estelle's cooking from out here," as they stepped into the house. Estelle heard them and came in from the kitchen with a big smile and open arms. "Uncle James, so great to see you, and I cannot thank you enough for coming down. And you must be this Detective Brown we have heard so much about?"

"Vernon, please, Estelle."

"I told you not to bring anything, James; what's with the package?"

"Just a Philly Care Package Estelle; you know, soft pretzels, TastyKakes, Peanut Chews, Zitner's candy, and Hope's Cookies; all the essentials."

"What, no Bassett's Ice Cream? What good are you? You know, James, we have TastyKakes down here now; we even have a Wawa over by the Cracker Barrel."

"I did see that. Everything smells great; I hope you did not go to too much trouble."

"Oh no, I lay out a spread like this every morning," she smiled.

The dining room table had been set for six, and the buffet had been laid out with fresh fruit, sausage and gravy, scrambled eggs, homemade biscuits, grits, bacon, and a sweet potato pie. There was a carafe of hot coffee on the table. Just as they contemplated loading their plates, Lincoln Anderson and his sister Tawana appeared, and more hugs and introductions ensued. Ten minutes later, plates were filled, and they all sat down to the feast. Dwight offered grace, and they all held hands and said, "Amen."

James asked, "Where do we want to start?"

Estelle replied, "Always family first; how is your family, and how has Bo come through his ordeal?"

"We are all good now, but it was a rough couple of months. Kids are resilient, as I'm sure you'll see, and Bo seems fine. He's playing a little ball this summer, but not nearly as much as the last three. And he's all set for Villanova in the Fall."

Unlike Lincoln Anderson, Bo Campbell was a highly recruited basketball player from Overbrook High School in Philadelphia. Future Stars had him ranked #1 at forward and #2 at guard. Last summer, he visited UCLA, Gonzaga, Kansas, Michigan, and Miami, then decided to stay close to home and enrolled at Villanova, much to his family's delight.

James asked, "Tawana, what's new with you? You have grown so much since I last saw you."

"All's good with me, Uncle James; my grades are pretty good, and I'm playing basketball and softball."

James McNeil suggested, "Lincoln, why not tell Vernon here the story of how you got recruited? This is a good one, Vern; it will remind you how God looks after His children."

"I'll try to make this real brief, Mr. Brown; the family has heard it so many times, they hear it in their sleep. But after a game last February, this white dude, Leonard Goldstein, comes up to us, introduces himself and his associate, and they come over the next morning for coffee. He owns this company, Future Stars; ever hear of it?"

"Absolutely, Lenny Goldstein is a legend in Philadelphia; did he tell you his Red Auerbach story?"

"No, but he told me I should be playing in college next year and asked me a few questions; then he drove up to Richmond Commonwealth and told Coach Blackwell about me. A week later, he came to see me play, and another week later, I'm going to RCU. Crazy, right?"

"The Good Lord is looking out for our family, and we won't let this little hiccup interfere with His plan, so bring us up to date on the situation," James said.

Dwight responded, "I think Estelle told you about the news conference our attorney held yesterday morning in front of the police station. Last night, a non-denominational memorial vigil was held at the sight of the incident. We went but stayed in the background. Good thing, I think, as some white guy started yelling, "Where's the Black kid who done this?" And then a Black guy responded with "Black Lives Matter," it could have gotten ugly, but the clergy appealed for civility, and the service broke up peacefully. I don't think it would take much to ignite this powder keg."

Vernon Brown decided to contribute, "Let's hope we can squelch that. I'd like to see the scene of the accident; can we do that this morning? I'm not here in any official capacity, so the police most likely won't provide me with anything; hopefully, your attorney can share whatever he has. Has he told you what the next step might be?"

"We can ride over to the scene after breakfast. We are not sure what the police's next step might be or if they are searching for anyone else. As of yesterday, they were not certain that the girl was even hit; she may just have fallen off her bike and hit her head. She was not wearing a helmet. I will try to reach Grimsley this morning and see if he knows anything more. He may also want to meet with you, Vernon. Do you think I should call Coach Blackwell?"

"Absolutely! He may already know, but it would be best if he hears it from you. Do it before we leave the house," Vernon answered.

More food, more coffee, more conversation; forty-five minutes later, the guys were in the car, heading to West End Boulevard.

Chapter 22

June 28th, Emporia

On the way over, Dwight reached both Coach Blackwell and Malcolm Grimsley. The coach had not heard about the accident and was appreciative of the call. He asked how he could help and asked to be kept advised.

Grimsley had not heard anything from the police, but he did not consider that unusual or problematic. He asked if they might stop by his office so they might strategize; he was glad to have Detective Brown on their team.

The crime scene now had yellow police tape as well as the flowers and candles from last evening's vigil. Without speaking, they all walked around the scene. Brown went up and down the street, looking to see the sightlines from both directions. He verified that you could not see into the drainage ditch just driving by it. How many cars might have driven past the bicycle just lying on the ground? He did not see anything else that the police might have missed, and he had seen enough.

As they got back into James's car, Brown said, "This is a horrible road to be riding a bike on; no shoulder or at all. Any driver the least bit distracted could have sideswiped this kid. But the driver certainly would have known he hit something, and it was still daylight, so he would have seen her or the bike in the mirror. Then again, a kid riding a bike might have been distracted by her cell phone and hit a rock or swerved to avoid something, losing control. I am anxious to learn what the bike might tell us."

Five minutes later, they were in downtown Emporia, as it was. There were no buildings more than two stories, nor any that appeared to have been built in the last seventy-five years. Grimsley's office was on South Main Street, as it appeared all the attorney offices were close to the Greensville County and Emporia City municipal offices and courts. There was a parking lot behind the building with plenty of available spaces.

"Something tells me I'm not in Philadelphia anymore," Brown commented.

"You noticed, huh, Vern?" James added.

Dwight Anderson led the way, and they walked up the one flight of stairs to the Law Offices of Grimsley and McDonald, LLC. It was a small suite that seemed to have private offices for the two attorneys, a conference room, and a utility room that served as a kitchen, mail, and supply room.

The offices were neat and clean but certainly not pretentious. In addition to the receptionist, there were two other women busy at their computers. The receptionist was expecting them and said, "Mr. Anderson?"

"That's me!"

She came out from behind her desk and said, "Please have seats in the conference room here," leading them into it. "Mr. Grimsley is on a call and will be right with you. May I offer you coffee? There is water right here."

They all agreed they had had enough coffee and politely declined.

Malcolm Grimsley soon joined them, and Dwight made the introductions. Not one for prolonged pleasantries, Grimsley said, "Thank you both for being here. Vernon, I'm sure your experience can prove helpful. Your role would be as our investigator. I am not certain how helpful the Emporia police will be, but we can dig a bit."

Vernon asked, "Just a couple of initial questions if I may, first, tell me about this police department; do they have detectives?"

"As you can imagine, it's a small force of officers and a Chief of Police. There is only one detective, but the County provides support when needed. Emporia is the seat of Greensville County. There are also Virginia State Police, mostly perusing I-95 for speeders."

"Did you receive a report as yet on the bike?"

"Just this morning, they confirmed the bike was struck, but there was no paint from the car; apparently, only the bumper hit the bike.

"Autopsy?"

"Scheduled for two today; preliminary said she most likely died from the fall, her head hitting a rock."

"Any CCTV cameras?"

"No such luck! Another two blocks on Main Street, there are cameras but only going North and South, so there is no view of the East-West traffic. Any vehicle that would have hit the Hennessey girls would have been traveling West to East."

James McNeil asked, "Just what is the racial vibe in this town, Malcolm?"

"Good question, James. Emporia has a population of 6,000, sixty-two percent Black and thirty percent White; we are governed by a City Council of seven elected members and a mayor. This is the Deep South, and we certainly have some rednecks and White Supremacists, but overall, I believe we peacefully coexist. Would you say that's fair, Dwight?"

"Nicely put, Malcolm, but the Police Department might be something else. I don't hear many nice things being said about the Chief, Walter Dukes."

Grimsley replied, "I agree, he's a mean SOB, and a couple of his officers are also."

Vernon Brown said, "So, do we have a plan? The autopsy report won't help much other than indicate whether she might have had drugs or alcohol in her system, or was raped, which appears unlikely as she was fully clothed. How can we find out if there are any witnesses who may be hesitant to come forward? Are there any Black police officers that I could speak to?"

Grimsley said, "I will talk to some of the Black church leaders, perhaps even Father Sullivan, and ask them to reach out to their parishioners. I'll also call two officers I know, Luke Blackwell and Booker Robinson, and ask them to talk to you."

Brown said, "That will be helpful, thanks, Malcolm. So, while we wait to see the next move the police take, we'll see if we can locate any witnesses or behind-the-scenes police scoop. It's the start of a plan."

Privately Brown wondered, just *why did the police so quickly decide that Lincoln Anderson was the perp?*

Chapter 23

June 14th, Brookline

Detectives Richard Duffy and Kathy Flanagan had been summoned into their Captain's office, and Detective Captain Henry Simon sat behind his desk as they entered and took seats. The office was nondescript, but with family pictures and many of Simon receiving commendations, it was cozy.

Simon himself was a twenty-five-year veteran of the force. At six feet three inches, he was still lean and muscular, thanks to a daily regimen of running and weight work. His hair was thinning but cut short. He was clean-shaven, and it suggested a daily grooming regimen.

He started, "Dick, Kathy, you can imagine the heat on this one! So where are you?"

Duffy, being the senior detective, took the lead, "I guess we should start with the medical update on the victim, Kelly Reynolds, and it's not encouraging. It seems like there may have been some fentanyl-laced in with Rohypnol causing further complications. The doctors are monitoring and hoping she might come out of the coma, but so far, nothing.

"We have completed all the interviews and really have not learned anything new or helpful. A good number of the kids saw Kelly dancing with this Tyler kid and going outside with him. He claims, and his three buddies confirm, that he came in, and they left together, and Kelly was still outside. While everyone saw Kelly, no one seemed to notice her drinking or hanging with any guys in particular, even though eight boys said they all danced with her at some point."

"Are we being stone-walled?"

"Absolutely, Cap! First, we know someone there did this, and it is quite likely that at least someone else was involved. Who saw what is difficult to say. I spoke this morning with Sergeant Johnson in the

Narc Unit, and he said he would try to find out about Rohypnol distribution. I had the same conversation with Angela Lopez in the SVU."

"Is the school able to appeal to the parents? Find what they might know about their kids' drug activity?"

"The Headmaster, Dr. Breckenridge, said he would make such an appeal, but he did not give us much hope that these wealthy people were going to turn in their kids for drug use and possible rape or murder. He thought pressure from us might be more effective. We did learn of six kids who had been suspended for possession, but only two of them were at the party, and so far, nothing that might implicate them."

"Kathy, you're awful quiet; cat got your tongue?"

"No, Cap, but as a rape victim, this whole subject just nauseates me; "Boys just having fun" is bullshit, pardon my French. Rape is rape, and to trivialize any form of it is disgusting. Now you have heard from me; sorry, Captain."

"No need to apologize; what's your next step?"

Duffy answered, "We are going to narrow down our list and re-interview the kids and the parents without the kids. Also, we are going to talk to other members of the faculty who were not at the party, just to get a feel for some of the boys. I think this is a house of cards, Cap; if one falls, the others may crumble. We need to find that weak link."

"Sounds good; you need anything from me? Nothing we are working on is more important."

"I think we are good for now, but will let you know if anything comes up; thanks, Cap."

Chapter 24

June 14th, Beth Israel Medical Center

The Reynolds family ordeal was near the end of its fourth day. Nothing really prepares anyone or any family to cope with a tragedy like this. Everyone tries to give you encouragement; "Keep the Faith," "God Loves Kelly," "Kelly is a fighter," but you know it is all bullshit. God lets kids die every day, even good kids who had families and friends praying for them. No, they preferred to rely on their doctors, not God, on this one.

Liz Reynolds had been unable to eat or sleep, and she looked it. She had circles around her eyes from crying and lack of sleep, her hair was unkempt, and the Prozac her doctor had prescribed was having minimal effect.

Her husband, Richard, the family rock, also appeared to be near the avalanche point. He wanted to be strong for his wife and son, but everyone had their breakpoint. No one was ever sure just when they might hit that low and how it would manifest itself, which only added to the anxiety.

Their son, Jack, a junior at Brown University, was home for the summer and had expected to intern at his dad's law firm. Jack was like his dad, usually strong under stress, but he had never experienced anything like this; this was not the SATs. But Jack was determined to show a strong face; caring for his sister was more than enough for them.

They tried to give each other breaks, but at least one would always remain in the room with Kelly.

They had visitors, Kelly's aunt and uncle, who lived in nearby Newton, Detectives Duffy and Flanagan, and school officials, but they were discouraging them from coming again. They would be in touch when anything changed.

Yesterday afternoon, they had a consultation with Dr. Roberts, and while their hopes were for good news, this was not the case. He told them that it appeared there was fentanyl laced with Rohypnol, causing further complications. They were allowing and hoping she might come out of the coma, but so far, nothing.

It was eleven-ten PM, and Elizabeth, Richards, and Jack Reynolds were sitting in Kelly's room with the hum of life-sustaining medical equipment as a backdrop. They had all nibbled at sandwiches and engaged in small talk while watching the bleeps and monitors.

Richard said, "Jack, why don't you take your mom home, and both of you get some rest? I'll remain and call should there be any changes."

"I guess we could try," Liz said for them both. "You look exhausted yourself, Richard."

"I am. I'll catnap here."

"What do you think, Jack? I'm sure you could use the break."

"Your call, mom."

Jack and Elizabeth started packing, but as they did, Dr. Roberts approached with an unidentified woman. Roberts was in his scrubs, the woman in a navy pantsuit. Both were wearing stoic expressions as they neared.

"Mr. and Mrs. Reynolds, and Jack, this is my associate, Dr. Sokoloff; may we sit with you, please?" as he pulled two chairs around to form a cluster with the Reynolds.

"What's wrong, doctor?" Liz Reynolds exclaimed as panic overtook her. Her husband took her hand but shared her fear.

"I'm sorry, but we have lost Kelly."

"NO!" Liz screamed, drawing eyes from the dozen bystanders and collapsing into her lap. Richard and Jack Reynolds did not know how to react and just sat dazed, looking back and forth from Liz to the doctors, who sat silently, allowing for the shock to set in.

"PLEASE TELL ME THIS IS NOT TRUE, DOCTOR!"

"I wish I could, but her brain function stopped an hour ago, and we have been unable to reverse it. Not that it matters, but the fentanyl was the most likely killer. I have never seen it mixed with Rohypnol; in fact, we cannot be certain that they were mixed. Throw in the alcohol, and it was a combination her body was unable to cope with. I'm so sorry!"

Jack and Richard had joined Liz in her sobbing, the three of them lost in their grief and disbelief. The doctors remained silent; there was nothing they could say at this point that would lessen the impact of their message.

Five minutes later, the previously unspoken Dr. Sokoloff said, "I know this is a terrible time to ask this, but Kelly's heart remains beating from the various life-sustaining equipment, and we would like to ask you to consider donating her organs."

This evoked another loud outburst from Liz Reynolds. *We have already moved from grief to decision-making*, she thought. *I hope Richard deals with that.*

Richard finally spoke, "Can you give us a few minutes to digest this? Give me your cell, Dr. Sokoloff; I'll call you. So, Kelly is still in her room?"

"She is! Let us know if you wish to visit. Again, we are all so sorry!"

With that, the doctors stood and slowly left.

Is this what it feels like when your world has ended? Look at these people, consumed in their own worlds, walking to visit a sick friend or relative, a nurse walking with a medicine tray to a patient's room, a fellow over there wondering if the Sox can beat the Yankees tonight, and a young woman intensely posting her daily selfie on Snapchat. WHAT THE FUCK IS WRONG WITH YOU PEOPLE? Don't you understand that our daughter just died? Our world has ended.

Richard Reynolds knew he'd need to keep it together and permit Liz to fall apart. There was no way for him to keep her from that darkness. Just be there, try to make the decisions that need to be made, keep her and Jack safe.

He finally said, "Let's go to Kelly's room; I'll call Dr. Sokoloff. We need to let her know about Kelly's organs."

Liz said, "Richard, I can't begin to think about it; I'll support whatever you decide."

"No, Liz; I'll tell you my thoughts, and you will say Yay or Nay; I am a firm believer in organ donation, and I believe if Kelly thought she might be able to save someone else's life, she would want that."

"I agree; you OK with that, Jack?" When he nodded his agreement, she said, "Please tell Dr. Sokoloff, and thank you, Richard."

Five minutes later, Dr. Sokoloff arrived and led them toward Kelly's room. Richard informed her of their decision. She said she would have the Authorizations prepared. They all walked very slowly into the room. Seeing Kelly triggered more bawling and tears; Richard noted, "The monitors are all still beeping; what's that about?"

Sokoloff replied, "The equipment is keeping the heart beating; the heart would stop immediately if we shut the equipment off, which we will do after your visit. I'll give you some privacy for a few minutes."

They collectively hugged Kelly, none trying to hold back tears. They hugged each other and held hands while Richard offered a prayer for Kelly's soul. Liz Reynolds would never pray to God again.

Five minutes later, Dr. Sokoloff returned with paperwork for them to sign. While doing this, she said, "Is there anyone I can call for you?"

Richard again, "No, we may call some family tonight, but otherwise, I'll make calls tomorrow. What happens now?"

"In the next day or so, you'll need to make arrangements with a funeral home; if you prefer, I'll call one for you, or you can have them call me. We will gather her belongings and return them to you or the funeral home. You can call me at any time about anything. If I do not hear from you before her funeral, I will reach out a couple of days later. There is nothing I can say that will not sound trite, but I really am so very sorry for your loss."

She led them back to the lobby and hugged them all.

The world around them pretended to be carrying on; it seemed so unfair.

Chapter 25

June 15th, Brookline

Detective Richard Duffy had his alarm set for seven, but at six-fifteen, his cell phone woke him. *Shit, it's the captain; this can't be good news!*

Duffy picks up his phone and scrambles to the bathroom, hoping to avoid waking his wife, "Hey Cap, good morning!"

"Not waking you, am I?"

Ignoring the question, "What's up?"

"Nothing good; Kelly Reynolds died last night."

"Ah, shit! I thought they expected her to recover?"

"The fentanyl was the wild card, but I don't have any details. I hope you and Flanagan can head down to the hospital this morning and get the details. The already high level of heat will be increased to broil level now that this is a murder investigation, Duff."

"I'm on it, Cap. We'll come in after the hospital and discuss the plan. Is the media reporting it yet?"

"Not yet; we got a message from hospital security late last night, but the public message will be handled by the media department this morning. We might have an hour or two head start."

"Talk to you later!"

When he returned to the bedroom, his wife, Shannon, was putting on her nightgown; "Not good news, I assume?"

"No such luck; that teenager from the graduation party died last night."

"Oh no; I just cannot imagine. I'll have coffee ready for you and Kathy; got time to eat anything?"

"Nah, I'll grab something at the hospital or on the way to the station afterward. Thanks, Hon!"

Twenty minutes later, Duffy had called Kathy Flanagan, dressed, kissed his wife, and had two cups of coffee as he climbed into his car.

They pulled into the parking lot outside the Emergency Room at seven-fifteen and walked into the relatively quiet ER. Flashing his badge and whispering as he approached the window, Duffy said, "We need to see someone about Kelly Reynolds, who died last evening."

"Just a sec, please, while I find out who might be available."

She made several calls and then said, "Detectives, Dr. Sokoloff just walked in, and she said you can go down to her office. If you go down that hall to the dead end, turn right, she's in the third office on your left."

"Thank you!" as they headed down the hall.

Dr. Sokoloff came out to greet them and showed them into her office. She had her Keurig coffee maker working and asked, "Can I offer you a cup?"

"No thanks, we had a cup on the way over. What can you tell us?"

"Dr. Roberts and I delivered the news to the family here last night at about eleven-fifteen. Kelly's brain function had ceased about an hour earlier. Obviously, they were devastated."

"We thought she was expected to recover."

"I think we all had hoped for that; rarely is the Rohypnol and alcohol mix fatal, but when fentanyl was added to the mix, the game changed."

"Where is her body, now?"

"Down in our morgue, but your Medical Examiner's team will be removing it this morning for an autopsy."

"Do you know any more about the addition of fentanyl?"

"We do not. We cannot say for certain that the Rohypnol had been laced with it or whether she took that separately. Perhaps the ME will be able to determine that."

"When should we expect the media to find out about it?" Flanagan asked.

She looked at her watch. "Marsha Littleton is our Director of Communications. She usually gets in around eight, reviews the various overnight emails, and then sends out a media briefing of anything appropriate. She would certainly include Kelly's death. So, the world should know by nine. She will not hold a news conference, though; that will be up to you and the family. If the hospital is requested to take part, Marsha would do so."

Duffy suggested, "Might you call the Reynolds and let them know of this timing? They might want to reach some family before this hits social media."

"Good idea; thanks."

"Has anyone from the school been notified?" Flanagan asked.

Sokoloff replied, "Yes, I spoke briefly last night with Colleen Lassiter."

They all stood; Duffy said, "Thanks for your time, Doctor. We'll be back in touch if anything comes up. We can find our way out."

"Good luck, officers, finding out who did this!"

At nine-twenty that morning, Tyler Longenecker received a group text message from Billy Bender, Nathan Friedlander, and Sheldon Warner who were included in the group.

"Did you hear Kelly Reynolds died last night? What are we going to do?"

Tyler replied, "First, delete this text message, all of you; I'll pick you up in twenty minutes."

Shit, fuck! Tyler thought to himself.

Thirty minutes later, Tyler had picked up Nate, Billy, and Shelly, and he had driven them all in silence over to Olmstead Park. They parked on Pond Avenue and got out of the car.

They found two benches overlooking the Leverett Pond, and Tyler said, "This is fucked. We only wanted to have a little fun; this is serious shit."

Nate asked, "What happened? I thought this shit was supposed to be harmless."

Billy replied, "The Snapchat post indicated that fentanyl was in the mix; how did that happen? That's what killed her."

Tyler said, "You said, Shelly, it had an extra kick in it that would assure she would not remember anything. If that extra kick was fentanyl, we killed her."

"Look, I don't know what's in this shit. Has anyone told anyone about our involvement?" Shelly asked."

They all shrugged in the negative.

Tyler said, "Good; first, no emails or texts on this subject to anyone. At some point, the police might start confiscating everyone's cell phones. We have two options, it seems; the first is just to go dark, never, ever say a word to any living soul. The second would be for us to confess to the roofing and rape but claim complete innocence about fentanyl and her death."

Nate replied, "I'm no lawyer, but drugging and raping would still be a crime, and I think we would still be responsible for her death since we gave her the drugs. I think we just need to stonewall and pray."

"There is a third option," Billy added, "The three of us can turn you in, Tyler. You bought the drugs, put them in her drink, and raped her. We simply watched."

Tyler turned white! He wasn't sure that Billy was serious, but he never considered that. Nate and Shelly looked at Billy, then at Tyler. *Were they actually considering that?* Tyler wondered.

"Are you serious, Billy? This is what our friendship means to you?"

"I just said it was an option, Tyler; chill!"

"Well, let's remove it as an option. I promise you that if we get caught, I'll take full responsibility, but in the meantime, we just go dark. Cool?"

"I'm good with that, Ty!" Billy said.

Shelly and Nate nodded in agreement. They all put their hands together in solidarity, all for one.

Nate said, "We have to expect that we'll all be questioned again. We need to keep our story the same; *the three of us were out at the pool when Tyler and Kelly came out. We went back in to give them some privacy. Five minutes later, Tyler came in, and we decided to leave. Tyler told Debbie he was leaving with us; we said some goodbyes and left. We went to Billy's together and crashed there.* All good?

Three nods!

Tyler added, "Meanwhile, we need to try and act normally, go on with our summer plans, go to Kelly's funeral if there is one, and just not be weird. And remember, NO TEXTING! Let's go get something to eat."

Chapter 26

June 28th, Emporia

1:30 PM

After visiting Grimsley, Anderson, McNeil, and Brown returned to the Anderson home to re-group and have a light lunch. Lincoln and his mother joined them to see if there was an update.

Estelle said, "I called Lenny Goldstein this morning. I just wanted him to know what was going on; he's such a good man, and I really like him. He was unaware of the situation with Lincoln and appreciated my call. He asked if he should call Coach Blackwell, and I told him that was unnecessary, as we called him earlier. His only advice was not to let the cracker cops railroad us."

Brown said, "That was a good idea, Estelle. Goldstein is a good ally to have should we need one. Lincoln, I'd like to visit with your two friends from work. Might you contact them, see if they are working, or when I can meet with them?"

"Will do, Mr. Brown," and Lincoln took out his phone and left the room.

Just then, Dwight Anderson's phone rang, "Grimsley!" he said to James and Vernon before answering, "Yes, Malcolm; what's up?" A minute or two passed before Dwight said, "No hint as to his agenda? OK, we'll meet you there at two-fifteen," and hung up.

"That obviously was Grimsley. He got a call from the Police Chief asking for us to meet today *to 'See if we can work something out?'* No offense, but Grimsley thought it best if you and Vernon did not come with us."

"Understood!" James responded.

Vernon said, "If Lincoln's friends are available, this might be a good time to meet with them. And please remind Grimsley to get us the info on the couple of Black officers."

Lincoln returned to the room and said, "Breanna White is home; here is her address and phone number. Ron is working, but he'll be off at three-thirty and home by four. He said to text him first," handing Brown another note.

"Lincoln, you, me, and Mr. Grimsley are meeting the Police Chief in twenty minutes, and no, I don't know what it's about. Clean-up."

Ten minutes later, they all left the house together; James and Vernon were off to Breanna White's, and Lincoln and his dad were off to the police station.

Malcolm Grimsley was waiting to meet them in the parking lot and got out of his car when they pulled up. "Some ground rules, gentlemen," Grimsley said, "let's just listen, find out why we are here. If he asks any questions, I'll answer if appropriate. If I do not know the answer, I'll simply tell them that I need to confer with you. If we must make any decisions, I'll ask for a break so we can come outside and discuss. Clear?"

They both nodded as they entered the police station. They were directed to the Chief's office and were quickly taken into Chief Dukes'. He stood, came out from behind his desk, and said, "I'm Police Chief Walter Dukes; good to see you, Malcolm, and glad to meet you, Mr. Anderson, and Lincoln. Let's have a seat; can I get you anything?"

They all shook hands, took seats, and said no thanks to the drink offer. They sat quietly, allowing the Chief to lead the way.

"Terrible thing about the tragic death of the Hennessey girl. One must wonder why she was out on such a dangerous road; I have asked our officers to watch out for kids out there, and we are looking to put up signs out there saying, *NO BIKES PERMITTED.*"

Malcolm knew the Chief was just posturing, and he would just let him.

Finally, the Chief said, "We'd like to dispose of this if we can today; if Lincoln here confesses to Negligent Homicide, we will drop any drug charges and plead for no jail time, just a year or two of probation."

Silence!

Grimsley wanted the Chief to believe they might consider this ridiculous offer. Grimsley thinks to himself *that the Chief knows Lincoln is innocent, but if he simply drops the charges, he'll have to continue the investigation for the real driver or refer the case to the County Detectives. He just wants this over; why?*

After an uncomfortable few minutes, Grimsley replies, "Just why is this a good idea for us to consider, Chief? I believe we have made this perfectly clear that Lincoln did not hit that poor girl and is the Good Samaritan here."

"I am not certain the jury would agree that Mr. Anderson here is simply a Good Samaritan, and with the drug possession, do you want to take that risk?"

"Chief Dukes, I believe the greater risk for the Andersons is to accept this deal, leaving him with a police record, jeopardizing this college scholarship, and potentially opening a civil suit. Might I counter-offer with your dropping all charges against my client?"

"That's not going to happen, Malcolm. Do you care to discuss this with your client?"

Grimsley asked the Andersons, "Do you want to discuss this outside?"

"No! We will not confess to something we did not do, period!" Dwight Anderson responded.

Grimsley asked, "Are we done here?"

"Not quite," Dukes replied, standing and walking back to his desk. He picked up his phone, "Jane, would you send in Officers Abbott and Wilkins, please?" hanging up the phone.

The office door opened, and the two officers who had roughed up Lincoln three days ago entered, one holding handcuffs, the other said, *"Lincoln Anderson, please stand and turn around. You are being charged with involuntary manslaughter in the death of Vicky Hennessey and drug possession. You have the right to remain silent. Anything you say can and will be used against you in a court of law. You have the right to an attorney. If you cannot afford an attorney, one will be provided for you. Do you understand the rights I have just read to you? With these rights in mind, do you wish to speak to me?"*

Lincoln stood, looked at his dad, then Grimsley, "Is this shit really happening to me? Can't you do anything? This is all bullshit, y'all know it." Tears started trickling down his cheeks as the officer snapped closed the handcuffs.

"Where are you taking my son?"

Dukes answered, "Over to the County Court House; we will arrange for a Pre-Arraignment Hearing within the hour."

"This is going to come down hard on you, Dukes. I have never seen a more trumped-up, bullshit case in my life. I am embarrassed for the good people of Emporia. Lincoln, we will meet you over at the Courthouse; try not to worry."

Lincoln was led out by Abbott and Wilkins; Dwight Anderson took a step toward Dukes and was grabbed by Grimsley, who whispered, "Easy, Dwight; we will deal with this cracker, but right now, we need to focus on Lincoln." He led Dwight out of the office without a word to the Chief, and they continued out of the building to the parking lot.

When he got seated in the car, Grimsley called his office, "Gloria, here we go again; please set up a Zoom meeting with every Black Church and civic leader in Greenville County for five tonight. The subject is the unlawful and tragic arrest of Lincoln Anderson. No, I'll call Diane Witherspoon myself; thanks!"

Part 4

Chapter 27

June 15th, Brookline

Detectives Duffy and Flanagan returned to the station with a minimum of conversation. Flanagan had called ahead to Captain Simon's office and told his assistant they were on the way in. When they arrived, she said, "He's waiting for you; you can go in."

"Have a seat; did you learn anything helpful?" Simon asked.

Duffy replied, "Not much that will help the investigation. The doctor tells us that the fentanyl made the Rohypnol and alcohol cocktail unstable. The media and social media, most likely, have been notified by now. We asked the hospital to alert Mr. and Mrs. Reynolds."

"Do you have a plan?" Simon asked.

"Looking at what we do know, the doer is one of the fifty or so boys who attended the party, so that narrows the list of suspects."

Simon interrupted, "Have we eliminated the Club staff and servers?"

Duffy replied, "It's hard to imagine that Kelly would have wandered off to the cabana with a stranger. We intend to talk to some of them again as to what they may have seen, especially the one server who got the first tip about Kelly sleeping in the cabana. The girl who gave her the tip might have seen more. This girl has not stepped forward for some reason. We'll ask the Club if they have background checks on the staff; if not, we can work on that."

Flanagan added, "We also thought we would explore the drug angle and see if we can identify who may have supplied or bought the roofie and fentanyl."

Duffy said, "Other than that, Cap, we'll try to re-interview many of the kids without their parents present, and some of the parents without the kids. I would hope to have a Top Ten suspect list within a day or two, then we can start drilling down on those kids."

"What kind of help do you need? This is a priority, and I'll find you some bodies."

"It would be a great help if someone else could re-interview the girls and the Club Staff and do background checks on the staff if needed."

Captain Simon asked, "How about the school administration, perhaps teachers who may have been there, and the chaperones? Kelly might have felt comfortable walking off with an adult she knew."

Duffy replied, "But unlikely, Cap, as I don't believe the killer knew the dosage would kill her. Thus, they ran the risk that she might be able to identify them upon waking."

"But wouldn't the boys be taking that same risk?"

"Not really; if Kelly says the last thing she remembers is taking a walk with Tyler Longenecker, that would be much different than taking a walk with Dr. Breckenridge."

"That makes sense; we OK then?"

"Think so, Cap; we'll keep you posted."

They retreated from Captain Simon's office and returned to their desks. Kathy Flanagan asked, "First step?"

"You call the school, talk to the Chief of Security re drugs, known users, suppliers, whatever you can learn. Also, find out if the staff is there during the summer or how to reach them if needed. I'm going to start working on that Top Ten list and setting up visits with the kids and parents. Some of these rich kids may be taking off to places unknown for the summer, so I think we need to jump on this. I want to give the Reynolds family a day or two, but we'll want to visit with them again about Kelly's friends. Thanks, Kathy!"

Chapter 28

Two hours later, they were in Duffy's car on their way to the Longenecker home. Duffy said, "How'd you make out on your calls?"

"OK! I connected with the Chief of Security, Anthony D'Amico. He gave me rough estimates on alcohol and drug use: ninety percent alcohol, fifty percent marijuana, fifteen percent more dangerous drugs. He gave me ten names, eight boys and two girls, he knows, or suspects are in that last category. All ten have been given warnings, and another offense would result in expulsion. He was unaware of the suppliers. I also spoke with Colleen Lassiter at the school, who said the senior staff works all summer, but of course, many took two and three-week, or more, vacations. She said that Doctor Breckenridge would be at his home on Nantucket most of the summer but was available for calls or Zooms."

"Good start, Kathy; perhaps one of those ten might be able to give up a supplier. I'm not expecting Everett Longenecker to be here, but his wife and Tyler will be. After this, we are going to speak again with Debbie Gibson. If OK with you, I'll take the lead again; you'll take notes?"

"I'm good with that Duff; thanks for asking if that is what you were doing."

They parked in the circular drive and knocked. Mrs. Longenecker herself answered the door. "Please come in, Detectives," leading them to the same sitting room they had been in previously and found Tyler waiting for them. All six feet, seven of him stood and shook their hands. Clearly, Tyler was more uncomfortable than on their last visit. He had a pained expression on his face and was avoiding eye contact.

Duffy said, "Thanks for seeing us again; we just have some follow-up questions for Tyler. If it is OK with you, Mrs. Longenecker, we'd like to speak with Tyler alone. Kids are often more apt to speak more freely when their parents are not listening."

"I guess that's OK; my husband suggested I sit in, but Tyler, if you are OK, I'm sure it's fine."

"I'll be fine, Mom," unconvincingly, trying to convince her.

She left, closing the door behind her.

Trying to get Tyler to relax a bit, "Duffy asked, "Any big plans for the summer, Tyler?"

"Actually, we do; we've got a place on the Cape, and we'll spend two or three weeks there, then my dad and I will come back, and I'll be doing something in his office. Mid-August, I'm spending three days down at Duke, where I'll be going in the Fall."

"Wow, sounds like fun. As I mentioned to your mom, we have a couple of follow-up questions, so we'll try not to take too much of your time. First, I'm assuming, and perhaps I shouldn't, but do you know that Kelly Reynolds died last night?"

"I did learn that this morning; that's just horrible. I cannot imagine what her mom and dad are going through."

"This is now a murder investigation, and we know that one or more of the boys at the party did this. Have you heard or seen anything on social media that might help us?"

"Haven't heard a thing; a lot of expressions of sympathy but no clues or speculation who might have done it."

"Several kids said you may have been the last person to see her. You mentioned walking outside with her around ten?"

"I think it was between nine-thirty and ten, but I doubt I was the last person to see her, and how would I know? I went inside, and Kelly was fine then."

"So, have you heard of any roofing at school, parties, whatever?"

"I did hear of one, I think, a year ago, but I do not know any details or who was involved."

"Do you know where kids at school get drugs? Is it another student or someone outside? This is why I didn't want your mom here, so you can feel free to speak."

"I'll admit to using weed on occasion, but my friends always seem to have it. I give them a couple of bucks, but I do not ask questions. And, since my mom is not here, I can tell you I have tried Oxy and even cocaine twice, but that was it."

"Can you think of any guys that might have been interested in Kelly romantically and she may have rejected?"

"I told you before that Kelly had a boyfriend a year or so ago, but I think his family moved to Hartford. I don't think she had a boyfriend since then, even though she may have gone on some dates. And I'm sure a lot of guys fantasized about Kelly; she was totally hot, but I'm not aware of anyone she rejected or was out to hurt her."

"Anything else you can think of Tyler?"

"No, not really."

"Kathy?"

"I'm good!"

Duffy said as he stood, "Thanks, Tyler; enjoy your summer. If you do hear any scuttlebutt, we would appreciate a call. Could we see your mom before we leave?"

A very much relieved Tyler said, "Sure, I'll get her, thanks."

Mrs. Longenecker returned and asked, "Everything OK?"

"Yes, fine; when do you expect your husband?" Duffy asked.

"Four, four-thirty."

"We'll call if we want to come back. I hope that is OK?"

"Sure!"

They left and debriefed in the car; "Well?" Duffy asked.

"I don't like the kid, but I didn't hear anything incriminating, you?"

"Only that he found Kelly 'totally hot.'"

Chapter 29

Duffy and Flanagan decided to drive over to the Gibsons to see if they could catch Debbie at home. Only one car in the drive, so it appeared at least someone was home.

Debbie Gibson answered the door herself, "Hello?" apparently not recognizing them.

"Hello, Debbie, Detectives Flanagan and Duffy again, may we come in, please?" Kathy Flanagan took the lead as prearranged.

"I guess so. But my mom and dad aren't home."

"That's OK; we have a couple of follow-up questions for you."

Debbie ushered them in, "This is Laura Forden; is it OK if she stays?"

"We'd like to speak with you alone; we'll only be a couple of minutes. Could Laura wait somewhere else, perhaps?"

"Laur, can you hang in my room for a few minutes?"

Laura went up the staircase, and they all took a seat in the sitting room.

"Thanks, Laura," Flanagan continued, "I guess you know by now that Kelly Reynolds died last night."

"Yeah, we all heard; SO horrible; do you know who did it yet?"

"We're working on it. Do you know any of the girls who were roofied in the last year at school?"

"Yes, but only by name, not personally."

"And the boys who raped them?"

"Yes!"

"Are you aware of any other cases the school officials may not be or boys who might have a supply of roofies?"

"No to both questions."

"How about you and Tyler and his friends Nate, Billy, and Sheldon? What have you been using?"

"Look, I think you asked this the last time; my parents know that I occasionally do some weed, and they are OK with it so long as I am not driving. I have also tried Oxy, but I'm not a regular user. Tyler and his buddies are more experimental, and I know they have tried coke and, I'm sure, some other stuff, but that's about all I can tell you."

"Any idea where any of these kids get their stuff?"

"It just seems that someone always has something. If I want weed, Tyler always has it. I see Tyler getting some stuff from Shelly. But I have no idea who the source is."

Duffy asked, "Have you spoken with Tyler since the party?"

"No, but we did text this morning about Kelly's death."

"Anything particular?"

"No, he just wanted to know if I had heard it."

Standing and handing her a card, Flanagan asked, "Thanks, Debbie; if you hear anything more on the school grapevine, please let me know. I'm sure we all want to solve this mystery."

"Will do; thanks, officers."

Duffy and Flanagan got into the car, and seeing that it was four-fifteen, Duffy asked, "Would you call the Longeneckers, Kathy, see if Mr. Longenecker is home yet?"

Kathy did, and Lindsay Longenecker said her husband had just gotten in. Kathy told her that they would be there in ten minutes.

Everett Longenecker himself met them at the door. "Please come in, Detectives; I heard you spoke with Tyler this morning in my absence." It was not a question and had a tone of disapproval.

"We did," Duffy replied, neither explaining nor apologizing. "We had a couple of more questions for you and your wife; we won't be long."

Longenecker showed them to the sitting room and yelled, "Lindsay, the detectives are here again."

"Be right there," came her reply.

And two minutes later, she joined them and took a seat.

Duffy resumed, "With Kelly Reynolds dying, we are asking more questions. Tyler told you we spoke with him this morning. What can you tell us about his alcohol and drug usage, and that of his friends?"

Mr. Longenecker clearly intended to answer all questions, "I'm not certain Tyler is any different than any other eighteen-year-old, detective. He has admitted marijuana use to us, and with it being legal now in much of the country, we have given our permission with the usual cautions. Other than that, detective, there is nothing more nefarious, I can assure you."

"And his friends?"

"I know nothing more. Lindsay?"

"The only thing I know is that Billy Bender does nothing, no weed nor alcohol. I think most of his other friends are about the same as Tyler; weed for sure, and hopefully nothing more."

Duffy then asked, "What can you tell us about his relationship with Debbie Gibson?"

Mr. Longenecker allowed his wife to take that one also, most likely not knowing much about his son's romantic life. "We like Debbie a lot, a really sweet girl from a good family. Tyler doesn't bring her around much, but we understand they were cooling it because of their college plans, and we certainly understand that."

Kathy Flanagan asked, "So you did not see marriage in their future?"

"While I know that can happen, I think it very difficult these days for high school romances to evolve into long-term happiness. There is just too much going on with kids and young adults these days."

Duffy and Flanagan looked at each other and seemed ready to leave when Everett Longenecker asked, "I've got one for you, detectives; are all the kids getting this much attention from you, or is Tyler more of a target?"

Duffy answered that one, "That's a fair question, Mr. Longenecker. Right now, it seems that Tyler might have been the last person to have been seen with Kelly, so yes, Tyler and his friends are getting a bit more scrutiny. But you and he have been quite helpful, and hopefully, we are done with you and him."

"Yes, it would be wonderful if you can find the perpetrator, and we can all move on."

Standing, Duffy said, "We all hope for that; thank you both again for your time and cooperation."

Everett Longenecker said to his wife, "I need to go back into the office; I have several more hours of prep for the Logan trial next week. If I see I'm going to be late, I'll stay in town."

"Oh, it's the Logan trial this time?"

"What's that supposed to mean, Lindsay?"

"You seem to spend two nights a week in town, or is that my imagination?"

"I'm not keeping track; that's apparently your job. Maintaining this lifestyle demands that I work long and hard; you're not offering to return to work, are you?"

With a tear in her eye and her lip quivering, Lindsay managed to say, "A discussion for another time, Everett."

Duffy and Flanagan returned to the car and pulled out of the driveway. Flanagan said to Duffy, "Funny how all these parents are now allowing weed and are convinced their kids are doing nothing more."

"It's always the other kids, Kath, never their own. I'll take you back to the station and then think we can call it a day."

Chapter 30

June 28th, Emporia

Felony criminal cases in Emporia were referred to the Greensville County Circuit Court, 6th Judicial Court, which was next door to the Emporia City Police and Court building.

Pre-Arraignment hearings were perfunctory, a simple reading of the charges against the defendant, the defendant's plea, and bail determination, if appropriate. No witnesses were called, nor evidence offered; that would come in a Preliminary trial scheduled within two weeks. The County Attorney's office usually sent one of their lower-level attorneys to argue against bail.

James McNeil and Vernon Brown joined Dwight Anderson and Malcolm Grimsley for this hearing. The CA's office had sent William Langley. There was a reporter from the local *Emporia Gazette* sitting in the back of the very small and drab courtroom. It was unclear whether he was here for this hearing or had been here all day.

It was three-twenty when the bailiff called, "All rise; the 6th Judicial Court of the Greensville County Circuit Court is now in session; the Honorable Margaret Fletcher presiding."

They all stood as Judge Fletcher traipsed into the courtroom. She was seventy-three years old, widowed, hard of hearing, and a strong law and order proponent. When she refused to retire, she was relegated to Pre-Arraignment and Pre-Trial hearings, yet she treated them all as if they were high-profile murder cases.

"All but the defendant, please be seated. Lincoln Anderson, you have been charged with Vehicular Manslaughter and possession of an illegal substance. How do you so plea?"

"Not guilty, your Honor."

"You may be seated. Mr. Langley, the vague charge complicates bail. Would you care to elaborate?"

Standing, Langley replied, "Yes, your honor; at this time, we are awaiting a determination of whether the defendant was impaired and request he be held without bail until such a determination is made. We should know that within twenty-four hours. Thank you, your Honor."

Malcolm Grimsley could barely contain his furor as he jumped up, "Your Honor, this is a travesty of justice. There is no evidence that Lincoln Anderson even touched the bicycle, let alone under the influence. My client is being railroaded here for some unknown reason."

Judge Fletcher ruled, "Since we will have our answer in twenty-four hours, we will hold the defendant until then. If he was not under the influence, bail would be permitted; if he were under the influence, he would be held until the Preliminary Hearing I'll schedule for this time, a week from today."

"This is an outrage, your Honor," Grimsley interrupted.

"We are adjourned," Judge Fletcher continued as she rose and exited the courtroom.

The bailiff came to remove Lincoln Anderson from the courtroom. His father hugged him, and Grimsley told Lincoln, "Don't worry Lincoln; we'll have you out tomorrow, but meanwhile, don't say a word to anyone, including to other inmates."

When Lincoln had been led out, Grimsley said, "Dwight, please call your wife and have her bring your daughter to my office for the five o'clock Zoom. We'll head there now. I am going to call for a protest tomorrow morning on the Courthouse steps."

"Do we really need to do that, Mal? He'll be out this time tomorrow?" Dwight asked.

"We do, Dwight. This will set the tone for the Preliminary hearing and for the treatment of all future falsely accused persons. We cannot allow this type of injustice."

With that, they left the courthouse for their respective cars and the short trip over to Grimsley's office.

Chapter 31

June 28th, Emporia

At five that evening, the Anderson family, along with James McNeil and Vernon Brown, stood behind Malcolm Grimsley. There was no smiling; Lincoln Anderson was being held in jail across the street. Grimsley had hired a local production company, so this would be a first-class presentation. Lincoln Anderson's trial was about to begin.

Grimsley began, "*Good evening, my brothers and sisters. I will not delay your dinner plans for long, and I appreciate y'all dialing in on this very important matter. First, let me introduce the Anderson family, Estelle and Dwight, and their children, Tawana and Dominique. We are joined here by Detective Vernon Brown of the Philadelphia Police Department, who is assisting us in an unofficial capacity, and James McNeil, an uncle of Estelle's. We thank them for being here.*

Noticeably missing is the Anderson's other son, Lincoln. Saturday afternoon, Lincoln was returning home from having a burger with two friends after their shift at Wendy's. After dropping the second friend off, he was heading home on West End Boulevard when he noticed a fallen bicycle off to the side of the road. Being the kind of kid Lincoln is, he stopped to see if anyone had fallen and needed assistance. He at once saw a girl in the drainage ditch who was not moving. She was later identified as Vicky Hennessy of Emporia, and I am sad to tell you she was dead at the scene.

Lincoln returned to his car and called 9-1-1. Ten minutes later, two white police officers arrived, put handcuffs on Lincoln, threw him to the ground, beat him, and planted drugs on him. They then took him to the police station, where they interviewed him with me and his father present. They let him go with the demand that he did not leave Emporia.

The next day, we were asked to come to the Police Chief's office, and Chief Walter Dukes suggested that Lincoln admit to Vehicular Homicide, and this would all go away with a suspended sentence. When we refused to admit to a crime Lincoln did not commit, Chief Dukes had Lincoln taken to the County jail, and an hour later, he had a Pre-Arraignment Hearing and was denied bail. As we stand here tonight, Lincoln Anderson, who did nothing except stop to see if he could offer aid to a fallen cyclist, is sitting in jail across the street.

My brothers and sisters, we cannot allow this police abuse of our Black population, and I am encouraging y'all to attend a protest on the steps of the County Courthouse tomorrow morning at nine o'clock. We must demand the release of Lincoln Anderson and fair treatment of all citizens who might be unfairly accused of a crime.

I hope to see y'all in the morning, and God Bless you!"

That was not the only conference going on that night. After Grimsley's Zoom. Commander Smith of the White Knights of the KKK in North Carolina reached Captain Jones of the Oath Keepers in Southern Virginia on their respective burner phones.

Smith said, "Hey, brother; did you catch that Zoom shit up there?"

"I did; what are we gonna do?"

"I'm not certain how many guys we can get by tomorrow morning to confront that rally, but we need to send a warning tonight. If you can manage that, I'll start mobilizing and perhaps have a demonstration of support for the police by tomorrow night. We'll talk again tomorrow morning after their rally. If those jigaboos want a war, we'll give them one."

Chapter 32

June 29th, Emporia

Two-fifteen AM

Mother Nature was calling Dwight Anderson for his middle-of-the-night constitution. He stood slowly, somewhat groggily, but was distracted by an orange glowing coming in the window. He walked over and nearly pooped himself as he saw a cross burning on their front lawn. He froze, barely being able to believe what he was seeing.

Coming quickly to his senses, he went to his closet and, using a step stool reached and retrieved the Sig Sauer P365 9mm semi-automatic he had bought five years ago, hoping he would never have to use it. To date, he hadn't.

"Estelle, get up quick and dial 9-1-1-there's a cross burning on our front lawn. Quick! I'm calling James right after I pee."

They both got in motion, deciding not to wake the children just yet. James said he and

Vernon would be there in ten, suggesting they await the police before venturing outside.

Eight minutes later, a police car pulled up with flashing lights but no sirens. Two Black officers, Luke Blackwell and Booker Robinson, jumped out of the car and drew their weapons. The flame was slowly burning out, but they walked towards it, searching for any discarded evidence. Dwight Anderson came out of the house, wielding his gun.

Blackwell seemed to be the senior officer and said, "Hey, Book, you want to check out back? Usually, these guys don't hang around but better to be safe."

Walking towards Dwight, Blackwell said, "You have a permit for that weapon, Mr. Anderson?"

"I do; thank you for getting here so quickly. May I ask your name?"

"I'm Officer Luke Blackwell, and my partner is Officer Booker Robinson. Can you tell me what happened here?"

"Not much of a story; I got up to go to the bathroom, and there was a glow in the window that drew my attention. I looked out and saw the burning cross. I woke my wife, grabbed my gun, and we made a couple of calls."

"May I ask who you called?"

"Yes! My wife's uncle is visiting from Philadelphia with a friend; speaking of the devil, here they are," as James and Vernon pulled up and parked behind the police car.

As Vernon and James approached, Robinson returned from the back, and Dwight suggested, "Why don't we go inside and talk this out? Knowing Estelle, she's got coffee going by now."

They went into the house, and Dwight was correct; the smell of brewing coffee permeated the house. They all sat down, and Estelle offered coffee; all gladly accepted, not concerned that it might interfere with their sleeping. Introductions were made, and Dwight repeated the brief story to James and Vernon.

Dwight started, "Officers, funny, not ha, ha funny but ironic funny, our attorney Malcolm Grimsley suggested Vernon Brown speak to you about the racial situation in town and on the force here. Do you know my son, Lincoln, is being held in the County jail for a crime he did not commit?"

Blackwell answered, "Yes, we are aware of your son's detainment. We were also made aware of the Zoom Press Conference and the appeal Mr. Grimsley made earlier this evening for a protest tomorrow morning. My guess is that this is a reminder to you that some white folks are looking. We are over our heads on this; in the morning, we'll make a report to the County's Hate Crime Unit, and I'm sure they will be in touch."

Vernon Brown asked, "Officers, do you have any idea just why the police were so quick to arrest and try to pin this on Lincoln? And yesterday, the Chief offered just to close the case if Lincoln would confess to hitting the girl. Is anyone still investigating this?"

Blackwell replied, "This might answer both questions; if Chief Dukes can resolve and close this quickly, he can avoid the County Detective Unit getting involved. So, at this point, I do not think there is an ongoing investigation, but that could change quickly now that you have not accepted that deal from Dukes."

Brown continued, "And what can you tell us about race relations in the police department?"

"Are we going off the record here?"

Brown nodded in the affirmative!

"This is my read, Booker can comment himself. By and large, I do not believe there's any serious problem within the department, meaning we get along well, might have beers after shifts, and have some family socializing. But, I said, by and large. I believe that there are four or five officers who are prejudiced and two that are outright racists. The Chief is an enigma to me; he seems to go whichever way the wind might blow. You see it differently, Book?"

"No! We've discussed this many times, and I agree with Luke."

James McNeil interjected, "Whom might we suspect lit the fire tonight?"

Robinson answered, "That's a tough one; this is the South, and as the country has learned in the last six years, hate is alive and well. The two largest groups are the White Knights of the KKK and the Oath Keepers, but there are many other splinter groups, some more extreme than others. Then you also have the lone rangers who are not part of a group but are just as dangerous."

Brown again, "So who are the two racists on your force?"

"You already met one, Jerry Abbott; the other is Caleb Barnes. Two SOBs," Blackwell responded.

They all looked around at each other. It seemed like they were talked out. Blackwell stood, showing that he believed the meeting was over, and offered, "I don't think there will be more trouble tonight, but who knows what tomorrow may bring, so stay alert. As I said, we'll refer this to the Hate Crimes Unit, and you will hear from them. And I would not be surprised if the County Detective Unit winds up getting involved, possibly as soon as tomorrow."

Dwight said, "Thanks again, Officers, for being so prompt and for the information you have given us. We will keep our conversation confidential. We all have an early day tomorrow."

They shook hands and thanked each other again. Vernon and James took off behind the police car. Dwight helped Estelle clean up, and they crawled back into bed, neither believing sleep would come anytime soon. His gun remained on Dwight's night table.

Chapter 33

June 16th, Brookline

Jeffrey Newman was a thirty-four-year-old science teacher at the Beaver Country Day School. He had been at BCDA for eight years now. He was popular with the students and staff and kept a low profile while still being affable and available to all.

After dating for two years, he married his wife, Taylor, five years ago, and they had a three-year-old daughter, Emily. Taylor was able to do some tutoring on a part-time basis now that Emily was old enough for preschool.

In high school, Newman started using weed because, well, wasn't everyone? While attending UMass, he progressed to Adderall and Ritalin, which helped his studying, the occasional Ecstasy for a good time at parties, and the even more occasional cocaine snort when offered. But Newman avoided heavy usage and the addictions that often followed; if there could be such a thing as a safe drug user, Jeff Newman could be that guy.

In his junior year in college, Newman started occasionally betting on sporting events, primarily college football and basketball. He did OK, winning slightly more than he lost, and post-college, added NFL and NBA gambling, rationalizing that his interest in watching sports was enhanced by his financial stake in the games. Online gambling made it even easier, and when he got married in 2017, Newman kept separate bank and credit card accounts for his activities.

By 2016, Newman was betting about $1,000 a week, which might not seem to be a lot, but that's $50,000 a year, and even if he won back half of it, that was still a $25,000 a year net expense. On a salary of $75,000 a year and his marriage plans imminent, he was fast approaching Armageddon.

What do they say about "When opportunity meets luck?"

Newman was talking to his old Fraternity Brother, Sean Reilly, who mentioned he was handling some drug distribution where he taught at Endicott College in Lynn, Massachusetts. He said he would make an introduction to his source, Skeets, in South Boston. One thing led to another, and Newman was now supplementing his teacher's salary, sometimes almost doubling it.

Newman would have one senior who would be his connection to the students. He would try to find successors in their sophomore or junior years. He had been running this side hustle now for five years with little or no issues.

Until Kelly Reynolds!

Using his burner phone, he texted Sheldon Warner, "Usual spot, ten-thirty."

The usual spot was the southeast corner of Philbrick Square. Just a small patch of land in the middle of a large Victorian residential community, it was never crowded, and if you could grab one of the two available benches, your privacy was guaranteed.

That was the case today as Warner and Newman parked within a minute of each other and met at the open bench. No exchange of pleasantries today, Newman said, "We both have a huge problem, Shelly. What can you tell me from your end?"

A perspiring and shaking Warner avoided eye contact with Newman, "All I know is that Tyler slipped her the roofie in a bottle of beer; none of us knew anything about the fentanyl; that seems to be the real problem."

"I talked to Skeets, and he said he was unaware of any fentanyl cocktail; he's having his inventory checked, but that's not going to help us. Who knows that you supplied Tyler with the stuff?"

"First, Mr. Newman, no one other than me, Billy, and Nate know that Tyler gave her the roofie. But the problem is that my customers all know that I, most likely, supplied the roofie to whoever gave it to her.

Once my name surfaces, I'm dead either way. And they'll want my list of customers and suppliers. You see it any differently?"

"Do Tyler, Billy, and Nate know that you and I are partners?"

"No way, Mr. Newman; you made that very clear to me a year ago."

"Good, Shelly; just lie low and let me know if you are contacted by the police again. I'll try to figure out something. Are you ok?"

"How can I be OK? I'm scared shitless; I'm afraid to talk to anyone, including my parents. I never thought this could happen."

"Just try not to panic; I'll get back to you soon."

They stood; Newman patted Shelly on the shoulder, and they walked to their cars.

Chapter 34

June 16th, Brookline

Detective Duffy hated spending time at headquarters; he always thought he should be out interviewing suspects, following leads, or searching for evidence. But even he realized that, at times, he needed to step back, take a breath, look at the evidence, and examine what may have been missed.

That's what he was doing all morning, and now he and Kathy Flanagan were staring at the murder board. They had narrowed down their suspect list to their Top Ten, as listed on the board:

Debbie Gibson, perhaps with some help

Tyler Longenecker

Nathan Friedlander

Billy Bender

Sheldon Warner

Chip Waters

Byron Delgrasso

Noah Lancaster

Jarrett Ashburn

Duffy said to Flanagan, "Want to talk these out again?"

"Never hurts, Duff. And the first thing we need to remember is that we are assuming that murder was never the intent. Our suspect most likely was only out to have some very sick fun or to embarrass Kelly Reynolds. If we want to consider pre-meditation, we will need a motive other than that."

"I agree, and that is why I still doubt Debbie Gibson was involved. There is no evidence that Tyler had any interest or a relationship with Reynolds before the party, despite his reference to her being 'totally hot.' But we must verify that with someone other than Debbie Gibson herself."

"Tyler and his buddies need to be on this list if for no other reason than Tyler was last seen with Kelly going outside," Flanagan said.

"Waters and Delgrasso were known to be drug users; apparently, this Lancaster is a total nut case, and Ashburn dated Kelly briefly in junior year and was known to have been hurt by the breakup. Are we missing anyone?"

"Don't think so, Duff, but our focus has been on students only; we agreed we also need to consider faculty, chaperones, and the Country Club staff."

"I think we need to split up. I'd like to go out to the Country Club, look around, and speak with Art Bowden and perhaps that server, Yvonne Hicks, again. Can I ask you to see if Colleen Lassiter is available at the school, and if so, talk to her about the faculty and chaperones? We are looking for any guys that might be known to use drugs or be romantically inclined. Good, Kathy?"

Yep, I'm on it!"

After calling and confirming Art Bowden's availability, Duffy pulled into The Country Club parking lot at three-fifty. The member lot had only a dozen or so cars. Summer afternoons were typically slow at all hot-weather clubs; those who were playing golf preferred the cooler mornings, but many members at TCC either vacationed or spent the summers on the Cape, Martha's Vineyard, or Nantucket.

Duffy was greeted by the receptionist; he identified himself and asked for Mr. Bowden. While waiting, he looked around the very plush club, and in a small room off the dining room, he noticed two tables of four women playing cards, or Maj Jong, he guessed.

Bowden interrupted his thinking and greeted him, "Detective, good to see you. Let's have a seat in the Men's Grill, can I offer you a drink?"

"A diet cola would be great, if not an inconvenience; thank you."

They took seats, and Bowden himself went behind the bar to get two drinks. Joining Duffy, he asked, "Still no arrest, detective? How might I help?"

"Not yet, but we like to think we are narrowing down the suspect list. First, is Yvonne Hicks around? I'd like to speak with her before I leave if I could."

"I'll check, but I think she usually does work weeknight dinners and would be in by four-thirty. "

"I also would like to walk around the grounds with you. I realize that with the golf course, it is a huge property, but I am wondering how accessible it might be for intruders. Is that an issue for you at all?"

"Not as much as you might think. First, many of the residents are members, and this is not a neighborhood known for rowdyism or vandalism," trying and failing not to sound condescending. Occasionally, some teenagers boost each other over the fence, but once they get over it, there is really nothing for them to do. They certainly are not going to golf, dine, or go swimming."

"OK, but if an intruder at night wanted to gain access, they could climb or cut the fence and at least get close to this building, if not into it?"

"Certainly possible, detective; let's go look around. Presumably, they would come by car, so if we walked a hundred or so yards down both sides, we'd cover the most accessible areas."

They exited through the Dining Room Terrace, and the outside patio looked over the 18th green on the golf course. They descended the steps to the beautifully landscaped and maintained gardens. They walked left towards the pool and tennis courts. This was most likely the path that Kelly would have taken on her fatal walk.

Duffy could see that the ten-foot fence would have been a deterrent to all but the most determined, and he would have to be quite agile or had a boost from a second perpetrator. If it were an undergraduate, he'd then have to join the party and seek out Kelly Reynolds casually.

All possible, Duffy thought to himself, but not likely. No, this attack came from a party attendee.

"I think I have seen enough, Mr. Bowden; let's return and see if Ms. Hicks has arrived, and I can let you get on with your day."

"No problem, detective; she should be in by now."

They returned the way they came as Duffy continued to look about the grounds. As they re-entered the dining room, Yvonne Hicks was in the dining room, perusing the table settings to make certain nothing was amiss, and everything was properly aligned.

"You are here, Yvonne. Good afternoon," Bowden called to her as she looked up. "Detective Duffy here had another question or two for you. I'll leave you two, and if I can help in any other way, detective, please feel free to call me."

"Thank you again, Mr. Bowden. I'll be brief, Ms. Hicks, as I only wanted to ask if you may have had any further recollection about our mystery woman or anything else at the party that night?"

"I have been racking my brain, detective, and the only other recollection was that this young lady was quite abrupt. She did not wait to see if I had any questions; she just moved on quickly heading out of the ballroom. With hindsight, I thought she might have taken me out to the cabana area or at least pointed to which one Ms. Reynolds was in. There are six cabanas out there. And then again, what took her out there in the first place? Did she look into all the cabanas?"

"Your questions are good ones, and we suspect that this girl knows more, but we do not know why she has not come forward. She may fear getting involved. I appreciate your time again, Ms. Hicks, I'll leave you to your work."

Duffy took leave and nodded to the receptionist, who spoke on the phone as he walked by. He returned to his car and placed a call to Kathy Flanagan. "Hey, Duff, how'd you make out?" she asked.

"OK, I guess, but nothing that will crack the case. I'm discounting the possibility that someone climbed the fence, joined the party, sought out, and escorted Kelly out to the cabana. That does not mean that an uninvited guest could not have walked through the front door and joined the party. I spoke briefly with Yvonne Hicks, who only added that she thought the young girl who told her about Kelly was quite abrupt and offered no help in finding her. This again supports our assumption that this mystery girl knows much more or was even involved in some way. You learn any more at the school?"

"Less than you, I fear. I reviewed each adult attendee at the party with Colleen Lassiter, and eight of the ten adults there were women, either school staff or faculty. The two men in attendance were faculty members, the Senior Class sponsor, and a foreign language teacher. I have their names, but Lassiter vouched for their character. I'll back-burner them for now. She also mentioned two thirtyish male teachers, one single and one wannabe single, whom she suspects flirts with the students, but neither was seen at the party.

Lastly, she said one of the students mentioned that the DJ, Eddie Walker, seemed to take a particular interest in Kelly Reynolds. I thought we might try to see him tomorrow; Lassiter gave me his address and phone number."

"Let's call it a day; want to have a drink?"

"Sorry, I got plans. Another time. See you in the morning, Duff!"

Duffy thought to himself, *perhaps I should call Cindy so as not to shock her; it's been a while since I was home early for dinner.*

Once she got over the initial shock, Duffy suggested they go out to eat. Twenty minutes later, they set out for LaMora, a popular Italian spot on Washington Street in Brookline. By eight o'clock, they were home, and the pasta and red wine had them both yawning. They watched one episode of *Suits* on Netflix, and by nine-thirty, they were both reading in bed.

Just after midnight, Duffy's Fitbit vibrated, showing he had a call coming in from Captain Simon. *Shit!* He climbed out of bed, grabbed his phone, and rushed into the bathroom, whispering, "Yeah, Cap, good news?"

"Don't we wish; I just got a call that they found a dead body in a car on Jordan Street, off Corey Road. According to his ID, the kid is Sheldon Warner; sound familiar?"

"You shitting me? Warner is one of Tyler Longenecker's buddies. Accident?"

"Unlikely that he got in the way of a stray bullet while sitting in his car."

"I'll call Kathy and get down there right away."

Sitting naked on the bed three feet away, Kathy Flanagan answered her cell phone.

Chapter 35

June 29th, Emporia

James McNeil and Vernon Brown had agreed to meet the Andersons and Malcolm Grimsley at eight AM at the County Courthouse. They gobbled down coffee and bagels in the hotel lobby and were in James's car by seven-fifty.

Traffic slowed about three blocks from the courthouse. *A traffic jam in downtown Emporia at eight o'clock on a summer weekday,* James thought to himself. Looking ahead, he could see a half dozen school buses, but *there ain't no school today.*

When they got within two blocks, they decided to park. They got out of the card and walked towards the courthouse. It did not take long to see they had plenty of company, as hordes of Blacks headed in the same direction, many carrying signs. *Grimsley wanted a big turnout; he looked like he would have one.*

The buses were unloading their passengers on Main Street and turning off to seek parking a block or two away. As they neared the courthouse, James and Vernon could see Grimsley at the top of the steps. He was orchestrating the set-up of a podium and microphones, and a half dozen chairs for someone. They were able to inch through the crowd and climb the steps. As they were greeting Grimsley, the Anderson family was coming up from the other direction.

The city and county had closed off the street a block away in each direction, but that was not going to be enough. Two fire engines had pulled onto the sidewalk in front of the courthouse steps to serve as a makeshift barrier. There were a dozen City and County uniformed police.

At eight-fifty-five, Grimsley tested the microphone again and was ready to speak. In addition to the Andersons, McNeil, and Brown, six church leaders, four Black and two white, were there to show solidarity. In a city of 3,600 Blacks, it would later be said that were more than double that in the streets of Emporia, Virginia. They had come from as far North as Richmond, South to Raleigh, North Carolina, and East to Norfolk. The local affiliates of CBS, NBC, ABC, and Fox News were represented, as were CNN and MSNBC.

No one knew what to expect, but no one wanted to miss it.

The increasingly impatient crowd was now chanting, *FREE LINCOLN A, FREE LINCOLN A, FREE LINCOLN A.* There were signs of all sizes, shapes, and tastes; several were questioning Police Chief Dukes' lineage.

Grimsley implored for silence and realized he had to start talking in hopes quiet would follow; *my fellow Emporians and our visitors from around the country. My name is Malcolm Grimsley, and I represent Lincoln Anderson, a young man falsely accused of murder and detained in this jail for no other reason than he stopped to see if he could provide assistance to a fallen young woman.* A chorus of boos came from the assembled, and some resumed the *FREE LINCOLN A* chant again.

Grimsley continued, Emporia has now joined other cities infamous for their unfair treatment of young Black children. I am asking Police Chief Dukes and Mayor Edgar Allen to come out now and speak to our concerns. Tell us what you intend to do about the systemic unfair treatment of Blacks in our fair city.

While we are waiting for the Mayor and Police Chief, I have invited the Reverend Moore of the Bible Baptist Church and Father Sullivan of St. Richards Catholic Church to say a few words.

Inside the courthouse, Mayor Allen, Chief Dukes, and County Administrator Isaiah Young sat drinking coffee, staring at the TV and several monitors from the security cameras outside the courthouse.

Allen stood and went out to the Men's Room for the third time in the last hour. Dukes was working his cell phone, texting with an officer who was a mile away, and said cars were still heading into town. Young was waiting to hear back from the Governor's office if the National Guard was available, 'just in case'.

Dukes asked, "Any ideas?"

"A question first," Young said, "Just why is this kid in jail in the first place?

"This could be Vehicular Homicide, Isaiah," Dukes replied.

"You have any evidence of that?" Young followed-up.

"Not yet; that's why we held him overnight. We've been in touch with the lab and pleaded for expedience."

"Was he given a breathalyzer?" Young asked.

Dukes replied, "Yes, that was negative, but you know they are notoriously unreliable."

Mayor Allen asked, "Would you have kept him if he was White?"

"Don't go all Woke on me now, Mr. Mayor."

Young said, "I guess letting the kid walk out there now is not an option?"

Dukes turned red, "How will that look? We gonna be dictated to by a mob?"

The mayor said, "OK, Walt, right now, we just don't want this to turn into another January 6th-like shitshow where they storm this building. How can we prevent that?"

"I hope the preachers out there can keep their people calm. We've called in another dozen or so City and County cops, and the State has an anti-riot force on its way. If things turn ugly, we use a fire hose first, then gas, and last resort, the riot team, but let's hope we don't get there."

Young asked, "So, neither of you plans to go out and make a statement?"

"Short of apologizing and releasing Anderson, I'm not sure anything either of us might say would appease them," the mayor answered. "The speeches seem to be winding down out there. Perhaps then the crowd will begin to disburse."

Just then, one of the cameras focused on a police car that had just started to burn, and it was attracting a crowd cheering *BURN BABY BURN*. So much for disbursing. The fire department unrolled the hose and dragged it towards the fire. But a block west on Main Street, the crowd overran three officers standing in front of a police car and torched that. With the crowd chanting for more, the situation was heading for an all-out riot.

The crowd sensed this also, and those who came for a peaceful demonstration quickly started to retreat in fear, parents dragging their children away.

Grimsley was appealing for calm, but the BURN BABY BURN calls were drowning him out. The church leaders had entered the crowd; they split up and were being escorted to the four remaining police cars.

Vernon Brown felt helpless, but now his primary concern was getting the Anderson family to safety. Random violence makes no distinction of its targets, and he quickly led them down the stairs and in the direction of their cars.

The crowd had not tried to breach the courthouse steps, and six armed guards stood watch from the top. Just then, a projectile was seen flying up from the crown toward the guards. Screams replaced chanting. The item turned out to be a Molotov Cocktail that landed midway up the steps and, with nothing to ignite, quickly burned out.

Inside, they had seen enough. The order was sent to the police on the ground to put on their gas masks and be prepared to ignite the Maximum Smoke Grenades they were carrying. Just the appearance of the masks sent much of the crowd dashing away from the courthouse. The order to *IGNITE* was given, and a half dozen explosions and blasts of gas were instantaneous. Screams and hasty retreats from the demonstrators followed. People were shielding their eyes and mouths. A father had to fight off the crowd to pick up his nine-year-old daughter, who had fallen and was crying hysterically.

The police and fire workers in their masks moved towards the crowd, herding them back down Main Street. The church leaders had been supplied masks and were trying to calmly encourage their flocks to disburse.

Just when it appeared things might be calming, a gunshot was heard, and a window on the second floor of the courthouse shattered. A second shot struck a window on the first floor. The police were searching for the source of the gunfire, but they saw no open windows or anyone on the rooftops.

The Chief looked at his phone and said, "The anti-Riot squad is five miles out. Our guys can hold until then."

At ten-forty, the smoke cleared, literally and figuratively. The crowd seemed to have had enough and was largely disbursed. The police were still on alert, searching for snipers or any troublemakers that might be lingering.

At eleven-twenty, the results of Lincoln Anderson's blood test were delivered to Chief Dukes, and by twelve-fifteen, he was released without bail.

Chapter 36

June 17th, Brookline

Duffy arrived at the Jordan Street crime scene at twelve-thirty AM but was far from the first on the scene. The Unis had blocked off the area, and traffic was unable to turn onto Jordan from Corey Street.

It was a warm evening and a clear night; a half-moon and a sky full of stars added to a surreal atmosphere. A crowd had gathered, and dog owners decided Fido could use another walk. More than half of the nearby homes had lights on, no doubt attracted by the bright lights outside. With the south side of Jordan under construction, only a half dozen homes on Jordan were close, but the homes on Corey were adding to the sightseers.

Three members of the forensics team were in the car; Dr. Lin Wang was examining the body while his two assistants were dusting and looking for any physical evidence that might have been left. Dr. Wang had asked the Unis to peruse the area for shell casings, cigarette butts, discarded soda cans, and anything that might have DNA or fingerprints.

Duffy crept up and was observing Wang's examination, hoping to disturb him enough to turn around, which he finally did.

"Detective Duffy, what brings you out on this delightful evening, as if I do not know. Gunshot wounds, two, from close range. Looks like a Glock 19, but I'll confirm that. Definitely fresh, within an hour or two at most. That's about all I can tell you for now, Duff."

Duffy had noticed Sargent Ortiz was directing the Unis and approached him, "Good evening, Sargent, I'm Detective Duffy. Have your officers interviewed any neighbors or these sightseers?"

"They have, and they have taken names and addresses should we want to re-interview, but no one seems to have seen or heard anything, except for one neighbor who thought he heard a couple of gunshots. Then he qualified that by saying he couldn't be sure because of the street noise from Corey Street."

"Good, thanks. After the car and body are removed, you might as well let your gang go; can they resume in daylight? I don't see any CCTV cameras around; could you ask the two or three closest neighbors if they have any security that can see the street? It's a long shot, but we can hope."

"Will do; I'll let you know what we come up with."

"Thanks, Sargent."

As Duffy turned away from Sargent Ortiz, he saw Kathy Flanagan quickly walking towards him.

"Hey Kath, how'd you get here so fast?"

"No traffic, flashers, you'd be surprised; whatta we got?"

"Not a robbery, definitely a hit. The question is whether it is related to Kelly Reynolds or was the kid in some other trouble. And you and I have the honor of going down the street and waking his family to this news."

"For this, I rushed down here?"

"Let's get this over with," Duffy said as they got into his car for the short drive down the street.

As they went further down the street, the neighborhood became much more fashionable, and when they got to 105, they had forgotten the rather drab duplexes only a block away. They pulled into the driveway and parked behind a late model Audi SUV in the drive. The home was a large Tudor with a brick façade and a two-car garage in the front of the house.

Noting all the lights off, Duffy said, "Shit, we'll have to wake them." They exited the car, closing the doors quietly. Flanagan knocked gently on the door; ten seconds later, she knocked a bit harder, trying to wake an adult, not the entire family. Duffy saw a light go on in an upstairs bedroom and a woman peek out the window.

She kept the chain on and opened the door two inches, "Hello, who is this?"

"Are you Mrs. Warner?" Duffy asked.

"Yes, who are you?"

"Detectives Duffy and Flanagan, Mrs. Warner," flashing both of their badges for her review. May we come in, please?"

"What's this about?"

"I'd rather discuss it with you inside, Mrs. Warner."

She opened the door, allowing them to enter. Mrs. Warner had thrown on a pink terry cloth robe and a pair of pink slippers. She was fiftyish and, even without makeup, was an attractive dark-haired woman.

"Now, can you tell me what this is about? Is this about my son?"

"It would be better if we could sit down, Mrs. Warner; is there anyone else at home?" Duffy asked.

She led them into the formal living room off the foyer as she answered, "My daughter is still sleeping; this isn't good, is it? Please?"

"No other way to tell you this, Mrs. Warner, but your son was killed in his car just up the street."

She collapsed in her seat, putting her face into her hands, and began sobbing. Kathy Flanagan moved her next to her and put her hand on her shoulder, offering her tissues. She was finally able to blurt, "Are you sure, officer?"

"Quite ma'am, white RAV4 and he had his wallet on him," Duffy replied.

"Was it an accident?"

"I'm afraid it's worse; he was shot."

Hearing this, the sobbing became more hysterical. Kathy said, "Can I get you anything, ma'am, water, wine? Is there anyone we can call for you?"

Warner shook her head, still unable to grasp what was happening.

Duffy said, "I can imagine how difficult this is, Mrs. Warner, but if we could ask you a couple of questions, it might help us track down who did this. Do you think you are up to it?"

She looked up at Duffy, "I'll try."

"Do you know if your son was having any problems, any enemies, any recent changes in his behavior?"

"I will take that wine now, officer; there's an open bottle in the fridge." She turned back to Duffy, "Nothing he chose to share, but these last few days, since that Reynolds girl died, he's been out of the house more than usual. I tried to talk to him about it, but he would only shrug. I don't even think he knew her that well, but I can understand the collective shock of all the kids."

"Do you know your son's friends or the ones he hung out with the most?"

"That's easy, Tyler Longenecker, Nate Friedlander, and Billy Bender." Kathy had returned with a glass of white wine, and Mrs. Warner paused for a sip. She needed both hands to hold the glass steady.

"I hate to ask this, but would you know if your son was using any drugs or other substances?"

"Does a parent ever know? I talked to him about it, but he would always dismiss me; I wouldn't be shocked, I guess. We hear stories about the school culture. But I do not know anything for certain."

Kathy asked, "Is there a Mr. Warner?"

"Yes, my ex-husband. He lives close by in Newton; I'll call him tonight."

"Is there someone else we might call for you to come and stay with you?" Kathy asked.

"I'll call my sister in the morning. She lives up in Manchester."

Duffy thought he had all he could get from her tonight. "Would you want us to call your ex for you? We can wait until someone gets here."

"That won't be necessary, officer. What happens now?"

"Your son was taken to the morgue in town; we will need you or your husband to come down in the morning to identify him. We will need to come back tomorrow with a forensics team to look at your son's room; does he have his own laptop?"

"Yes!"

"Please do not touch it; we have his cell phone. His car was towed and will be examined in the next day or two. With social media, I suspect by noon tomorrow, your son's death will be all over it, so you may want to have someone help you notify friends and family before then. We will talk to you in the morning and again Mrs. Warner; we are very sorry for your loss."

They all stood, Mrs. Warner still clutching her wine glass for comfort as she walked them to the door.

As they pulled away. Duffy said to Flanagan, "It never gets easier, does it, Kathy? I guess that's a good thing, huh?"

Chapter 37

June 17th, Brookline

It was eight-fifteen when Detective Duffy sauntered into the squad room with two coffees and a large box of munchkins. Kathy Flanagan was working at her computer and exchanged pleasantries. He delivered her coffee and offered her first dibs on the munchkins. She gratefully accepted both. He left his coffee on his desk, took three munchkins for himself, and took the box to the small kitchen area behind the squad room.

Returning, he picked up his coffee and rolled his chair over to Kathy's, "Whatta you got, anything?"

"I just wanted to see what the news was reporting; local news had the body found, but as yet, unidentified. I also am searching social media, but nothing there."

"Do you believe in coincidences?"

"Of course not, so we both assume this is related in some way to Kelly Reynolds' death?"

"Absolutely! This suggests that this Warner kid was the doer or certainly knew who the doer was and needed to be silenced. Any other possibilities?"

Kathy pondered that for a minute, finally adding, "A third possibility might be the source of the drugs; perhaps Warner knew who he or she was?"

"That's good, Kath. I spoke with Mrs. Warner on the way in, and she and her ex will be in at around nine. The forensics are out at her place now, so there is no need for us to go out there. I've got Radar looking at the kid's cell phone, and he said he would have something by ten. I think we need to get back with Longenecker, Friedlander, and Bender; those kids know more than they shared. Warner's phone can tell us other kids he might have contacted."

"While we are waiting for the Warners, I'll reach out to Colleen Lassiter at school and see what more she might know about Sheldon Warner. I'll also monitor local and social media for updates."

Colleen Lassiter had finished breakfast and was enjoying her second cup of coffee reading the Boston Globe when her cell phone rang. "Hello?" she answered.

"Hello, Colleen, this is Kathy Flanagan, Brookline Detective. Good morning; am I interrupting?"

"Oh, not really; what's up?"

"I'm not certain if you have heard as yet, but Sheldon Warner was murdered last night."

"Oh no! Do you think it is related to Kelly Reynolds?"

"We do, but we're not certain just how yet. What can you tell me about Sheldon that might help?"

"Not much; his parents divorced a couple of years back, and I know he struggled with that; his work suffered but had been better this past year. He gets average grades but is a bit rebellious and at times reveals a sharp temper."

"Oh, like what?"

"Last year, he told one of his teachers to go fuck himself and walked out of his class. I do not recall what it was about. Perhaps it is in his file."

"Not important, thanks! Might you ask around to the staff and faculty; we are still focusing on the drug issue, thinking he might have known something about the drugs that were given to Kelly?"

"I'll see what I can find out. Is that all?"

"For now, yes. Call me if you learn any more, and I'll get back to you if I need to reach others. Thank you, Colleen."

By ten o'clock, the Warners had come and gone, and the media was now reporting Warner's death. Duffy was reviewing the report off Sheldon Warner's cell phone. A lot of text messages but very few actual calls. The messages were all very benign between his friends and family, typical teen, "Hey, wassup, bruh." There were several messages going back two years, sent to an unidentified burner phone, with messages like, "five o'clock Tuesday, usual place," "We need to meet," and "All good?" Radar was tracking the service provider of the burner phone.

"Let's go," Duffy said to Flanagan.

"Where to?"

"Longeneckers"

"Giddyap!"

They both shut down their computers, locked their desk drawers, checked to make certain they had weapons, and took off.

"You again," an obviously perturbed Everett Longenecker asked as he opened the door for the two detectives. "What can we do for you this time?"

Duffy replied, "We just want to ask Tyler a few questions about Sheldon Warner. We assume you have heard?"

"We have, and we are all quite upset by it. Come in, and please have a seat while I fetch Tyler."

Duffy and Flanagan knew their way to the sitting room by now and were seated when Tyler and his father returned.

Duffy said, "Sorry about your friend's death, Tyler; we won't take long, but we do have a few questions, is that OK?"

Tyler, wearing a Duke tee shirt and athletic shorts, sat expressionless; his face was red, and to Duffy, it appeared he might have been crying. Tyler mumbled, "OK, I guess." His father had no intention of leaving Tyler alone to answer any questions.

Duffy asked, "Was Sheldon having any problems or beefs with anyone that might have led to this?"

"No more than the rest of us. I think we have all been stressed since that party and Kelly's death. I'm not aware of any dudes that might have had it in for Shel."

"Did Sheldon have a romantic interest or fascination with Kelly Reynolds?"

"Definitely not."

"Was he involved in illegal substances in any way?"

Tyler looked up. After a pregnant pause that Duffy took to be a tell, Tyler answered, "Like the rest of us, an occasional doobie, but nothing other than that. Can I ask why you would even think that?"

"Fair question, Tyler," Duffy replied. "At this point, we believe that Sheldon's death is related to Kelly Reynolds' death, and if so, it would suggest that Sheldon was somehow involved or knew who was. That might include whoever supplied the drugs to the rapist."

Everett Longenecker said, "Will that be all, detectives? Tyler has been more than cooperative. Please allow him to grieve his friend's death."

"One last question, if I may," Duffy said as he stood, "Where do you get your doobies when you are occasionally inclined to partake?"

"Someone always seems to have some, and yes, often it was Shel."

"Thank you both for your time," Duffy said as he and Kathy made their way to the door.

Chapter 38

June 29th, Emporia

Police Chief Walter Dukes sat in his office alone, just having consumed a tuna salad sandwich and diet coke at his desk.

Dukes was pissed! While he was glad that the near riot was quelled with no serious injuries or deaths, the investigation into the death of Vicki Hennessey would be shifted to the Detective Unit of Greensville County. Normally, Dukes would welcome shifting cases to the County, less work for his team, but there was something about this one that did not sit well with Dukes.

While a Pre-Trial Hearing had been scheduled for Lincoln Anderson, he wasn't convinced the County Attorney would pursue the charges. What evidence did they have? The kid was found at the scene of the crime. There was no damage to his car, no alcohol or drugs in his system, no witnesses or other physical evidence. The kid could have just driven off, and no one would have known he existed. That packet of weed didn't mean shit, and truth be told, he believed that Abbott might have planted it on the kid.

Commander Smith of the White Knights of the KKK in North Carolina and Captain Jones of the Oath Keepers in Virginia were on the phone again, discussing the protest and aftermath.

Smith asked, "What did you think?"

"I think if those crickets had their way, no one would be in jail. This country is fucked when you can protest and get criminals released. We need to restore law and order, brother. How many you got coming up for our parade tomorrow?"

"About seventy-five good citizens. We'll be coming in a convoy of fifteen pick-ups; we're meeting at the Days Inn in Roanoke Rapids at eight."

"Good, we'll plan to meet you at nine at the Walmart off the I-95 exit. And remember a hood for me; see you then. We'll show them what real Freedom Fighters look like."

"ORION, Brother Jones!"

County Administrator Isaiah Young scheduled a meeting with the Commonwealth's Attorney, Scott Atkins, and his Assistant, Vanessa Walker.

Greensville County is governed by a four-member Board of Supervisors who are elected to four-year terms. The County Administrator oversees the Board. Isaiah Young has served in this position for seven years.

The fifty-three-year-old Young is a native of Emporia. His family owns Young's Chrysler-Plymouth dealership, and he held several positions on the Board of the Emporia-Greensville Chamber of Commerce before being elected to the Board of Supervisors. The position demanded diplomacy in bringing together diverse personalities and interests. Young was liked by the people who counted in Greensville, the four Supervisors, the business community, and the voters.

At six feet, three inches, and two hundred sixty pounds, Young resembled an out-of-shape NFL linebacker. He was bald with a short, white-gray beard and mustache. His gray suit may have fit him ten years ago, but it was stretching at the seams today. Don't even suggest buttoning the jacket.

He was meeting with Atkins and Walker in the County's small conference room. The round table could hold six. There was a side table with a coffeemaker and fixings and several bottles of water. The window overlooked Main Street; the other walls had photographs of Emporia's scenic landscapes.

To get the meeting rolling, Young asked Atkins, "What are we going to do with this Anderson kid?"

"I honestly don't know Ike. I'm not even sure why he was arrested. Setting aside that itsy bit of weed, which is bullshit, the kid called in the body. There were no drugs or alcohol in his system. No evidence on his car or the girl's bike to indicate that it was him who hit her. But the bike was hit by someone. Did Chief Dukes search for or find any other possible vehicles?"

"No, he seemed quite content that this kid did it."

"If I may, Mr. Young," Vanessa Walker interjected, "With a deceased person, Emporia should have immediately turned the case over to us. I don't understand why Dukes kept it and considered it closed so quickly. Now we must investigate with the community already up in arms and the Preliminary Hearing six days away."

Atkins added, "Good observation, Vanessa, and if we drop the case too quickly, it will make the Emporia PD look bad, and Dukes will be pissed."

"I'm not too concerned with Dukes being pissed, Scott," Young responded. "I want to do the right thing for the Anderson kid and the Hennessey family. Let's see if our detectives can come up with anything in the next couple of days, and then we can reconvene before the hearing. Make sense?"

"Not much time, but this seems like the only option at this point. Thanks, Ike," Atkins replied, while Walker shook her head in agreement.

Chapter 39

June 17th, Brookline

After murdering Sheldon Warner last night, Jeff Newman went home and tried to quietly get into bed without waking his wife, Taylor. "You're late, Jeff!"

"Yeah, sorry, Harvey and I got interested in the Red Sox game and stayed at O'Shea's to the end of the game. I hope I didn't wake you."

The next morning, Jeff snuck out of the house early, leaving a note for Taylor that he was heading to the gym and then breakfast with Harvey.

But instead, he drove out to the Allerton Overlook. He parked and locked the car and found a bench in a quiet spot. He had already taken a Ritalin tablet and took the first sip of an Old Forester pint he bought last night.

Jeff struggled to maintain his sanity amidst the weight of his dark secret. The ghost of Sheldon Warner appeared in his dreams last night. On the way over this morning, Warner whispered accusations in his ear. Paranoia set in as Newman becomes convinced that he cannot keep this a secret. He has now added murder to drugs and gambling on his rap sheet.

Where did it go wrong? Newman thought to himself. *I'm one of the good guys, educated, a good teacher, a faithful and loving husband and father.* He seemed unwilling to accept that he was a victim of his own decisions and was driven by greed.

Can I believe no one else in the school knew I was supplying Warner with his drugs? He wondered. *And that $5,000 I lost last night on the Sox game was money I owed Skeets for the last fentanyl delivery. He'll have to wait.*

He needed to stay calm, act normally, and protect Taylor and Emily. Then he wondered who was pitching for the Sox tonight.

Chapter 40

June 17th, Brookline

It was eleven-twenty when Detectives Duffy and Flanagan left the Longeneckers. After Duffy pulled out of the driveway, he asked, "Do you agree it looks like the Warner kid was moving the drugs?"

"Definitely, but now that he's dead, we do not know whom he may have supplied what for the party. His killer is either the person who gave it to Kelly or, possibly, the supplier from which Warner got his drugs."

"I agree, Kath, but my guess is the latter. I don't see a rich white kid firing rounds into a car at midnight. We must start squeezing some of these kids about where they get their drugs. We can give them immunity, and we simply want to know the source of the drugs. One or two more kids like Warner may be making some side money to supplement Daddy's allowance. And if we can get to those kids, maybe they lead us to the supplier."

"Warner's death aside, boss, this is a huge break for us as we can now focus on Warner, his friends, family, and contacts."

"Speaking of food, how about an early lunch? We're driving right by Virginia's."

"Good by me."

Five minutes later, they parked and entered Virginia's, an upscale sandwich shop, where sleek marble countertops perfectly complement the warm wooden furnishings. The neatly arranged shelves are adorned with artisanal breads and gourmet ingredients. The air is filled with the aroma of freshly baked bread and sizzling meats, enticing patrons to indulge in their culinary desires.

It was early, so only two other tables were occupied. Duffy led to a table in the far corner. While they both had the menu memorized, they quickly perused it while waiting for a server to take the order. When she arrived, Flanagan ordered chicken salad, Duffy the roast beef, and they both ordered Diet Cokes.

When the server left, Duffy had his opening, "Anything you want to tell me, Kathy?"

"That's an open-ended question, boss. You want the five-day weather forecast, my Red Sox predictions, or some houses for sale on the Cape?"

"Wise ass! I was thinking more about business, office gossip?"

"Sorry, Duff, I am out of that loop."

"You're going to make this difficult? I meant about you and the captain."

Kathy looked up, stone-faced. *Shit*, she thought. *Does he know, or is he fishing?* "What do you mean, Duff? That's quite open-ended also."

"OK, Kath! The other night, Price called me to tell me of Warner's murder. Ten seconds later, I called you to tell you the same. And by some huge coincidence, you and he had Jimmy Kimmel on your TVs. And when I asked you how you got to the scene so quickly, you told me the traffic was light. And I know Price keeps an apartment close to the station for those late nights he chooses not to drive home to Framingham."

Nailed! Can I lie my way out of this, or do I confess? Kathy stared at her partner as if he might change the subject. She glanced over her shoulder, hoping for a food delivery interruption. She cracked her knuckles and took a sip of her Coke. "You got me, Duff. What can I say?"

"You could tell me just what the fuck is wrong with you? You are sleeping with your married boss. Do you think this is a wise career move? How long has this been going on, may I ask?"

"About a month. It's nothing we planned. It just sort of happened."

"Affairs don't just sorta happen, Kathy. One person initiates it, and the other goes along with it. And it doesn't really matter which of you did what. Do you have a plan? Are you in love with the guy and believe he will divorce his wife, and you two will live happily ever after?"

"OK, Duff. You have made your point crystal clear. I don't have any answers for you. Can I ask for your confidentiality while I sort this out?"

"Call me old-fashioned Kathy, but I don't like this. I will respect your confidence for now, but not, as you say, open-ended."

Thankfully, the server delivered their sandwiches and refilled their Cokes. They played with the mustard and mayo, dug in, and ate quickly in silence.

Part 5

145

Chapter 41

June 30th, Emporia

James and Vernon decided to get out of the hotel for breakfast and found themselves at the nearby *Cracker Barrel*. Like every other *Cracker Barrel* in the world, you entered into their gift shop where you could buy anything you hadn't seen in the last fifty years. That included candy, where you could still buy *Clark Bars and Necco Wafers*.

"You need any other reminders that we are not in Philly anymore, Vern?" asked James.

"Nah, I suspect scrapple ain't on the menu, huh?

They were shown to a table by an elderly host who told them Juanita would be their server and she would be with them soon. They perused the menu but noted that, too, had not changed in the last fifty years either.

Juanita stopped by and introduced herself, and they both begged for black coffee.

"You going with your usual *Country Fried Steak* with biscuits and gravy?" Vernon asked.

"How'd you know, Vern? You doing the same?"

"No thanks, James, I do not need any laxative. Is it possible they don't have omelets on the menu?"

"I'm sure they'll be glad to make you one, but you might want to have a backup plan." Looking around the half-filled restaurant, James said, "Have you noticed, Vern, that we are the youngest people in here? I should come here more often."

Juanita returned with their coffee, and they learned that, in fact, "No sir, sorry, we do not have omelets." Vernon decided to opt for *French Toast with a side of bacon*. James went with the *Grandpa's Country Fried Breakfast*.

With that business concluded, Vernon said, "You think there's any chance we can get out of this place before Labor Day, James?"

"Yeah, Linda asked me the same thing last night. I hate leaving before this gets resolved, and we haven't helped much. We'll discuss it with Dwight and Estelle this morning. Did you connect with Grimsley last night?"

"I did, and he told me Luke Blackwell was working the night shift this week and could meet with us later this morning. I'll call him on the way over to the Campbells."

Juanita delivered their breakfast and refilled their coffee mugs. They got focused on chowing and catching up on their families at home. They were expected at the Andersons at nine-thirty, and at ten after, Vern looked at his watch and motioned to Juanita to bring their check, which she promptly did.

"I got this one, James," standing slowly and reaching into his pocket for his wallet.

"I'll take care of the tip," James replied, throwing a five-dollar bill on the table.

They got in the short line to the cashier, and James said to Vernon, "Last chance to get a couple of Moon Pies for the road."

James knew his way around town by now and took Atlantic Street to head south through town towards the Andersons. As they approached Main Street, there were three or four cars stopped in front of them at the traffic light. *A traffic jam in downtown Emporia*, James thought to himself. But when the light turned green and no one moved, Brown lowered his window and heard horns tooting, and saw what appeared to be a procession of pick-up trucks. *A parade of some sort* assumed Brown.

"Holy Shit," James exclaimed. "I ain't ever seen a parade where guys are wearing sheets, waving Confederate Flags, and carrying rifles. That's the Klan up there, Vern."

James called the Andersons, and Estelle answered. "Yeah, we know, James, they're showing it on local TV. You ain't seen the signs: *Justice for Vicki, Lynch Lincoln, and Trump 2024*? Just be careful up there; take your time. We'll see you whenever."

It appeared the last of the pick-up trucks had moved through the intersection, and traffic resumed at a crawl. Each car slowed down to look down Main Street. Vernon and James did the same. There were few onlookers on the sidewalk, perhaps not wanting to make things worse. Once they got over Main Street, James decided to go down to Center Street before he turned right. He pulled up in front of the Andersons at nine-forty.

Estelle and Dwight were sitting out on the front porch, and Vern and James joined them.

"Coffee, gentlemen?" Estelle asked.

"I'm coffee'd out, thanks," James replied.

"Ditto," Vernon added.

"Nice little town you got here," James offered sarcastically. "I think I like my chances in West Philly better."

Dwight replied, "Please don't judge all Emporians by a small gang of malcontented racists, guys. I'll bet most of them were not even from Emporia. And it's about ten percent of the support we had for our rally."

Brown wanted to get off that subject; "I spoke with Grimsley last night and Officer Blackwell on the way over here. We are meeting at eleven o'clock at the Dunkin Donuts off I-95, the next exit South. And then, at one o'clock, Assistant County Attorney Vanessa Walker agreed to meet with us even though she made it clear she might not be able to share much."

James added, "We are hopeful that after these meetings and a debriefing with y'all and Grimsley, we might head north back to Philly. We don't want to leave you hanging, but we will have gotten about as far as we can go, but we'll play it by ear."

Estelle responded, "We understand you wanna get back to your families and have appreciated your being here. When you gotta go, you gotta go. Thank you both. I hope you can come for dinner tonight; it's Fried Chicken night here at the Andersons."

James looked at Vernon, hoping for a sign of agreement. *Was that a wink or just a blink?* James said, "We'll be here at six, Estelle."

Rather than head back through town to get to I-95, they decided to just go down Route 301, which ran parallel to I-95. There were about a dozen cars in the Dunkin lot when they arrived. When they entered, it was easy to spot Luke Blackwell wearing the green and gold Norfolk State tee shirt he said he would.

He stood to greet them. He was about six foot two, two hundred pounds of medium black complexion, buzz cut hair, and a short beard. Vernon thought to himself he had some resemblance to Denzel Washington.

Vernon said, "Officer Blackwell? I'm Vernon Brown, and this is my friend and Lincoln Anderson's uncle, James McNeil."

They all shook hands. James asked, "Can we get you anything? Looks like you already have some coffee."

"I'm good, thanks."

"Vern?"

"If you're getting one for yourself, I'll have one. I'll share whatever donut you choose, and remember, they are sprinkles down here, not jimmies."

James walked to the counter, leaving Vernon with Blackwell. Vernon said to Blackwell, "Funny you would suggest Dunkin Donuts Luke, James, and I visit one in Philly almost once a week."

"It's just far enough away from Emporia that it's unlikely we'll be seen. I hope this is OK."

"Fine!"

James returned with two coffees and two chocolate-covered donuts with rainbow jimmies.

"I thought I said we would share one," Vernon said.

"I heard you, but I thought we could convince Luke here to join us."

"OK, you talked me into it; I'll take a half."

James asked Luke, "You grow up in this area, Luke?"

"Sort of, I guess. I grew up in the Wilson, North Carolina area; then, I went to Norfolk State and, after getting a Master's in Criminal Justice there, joined the Emporia Police Department. Six months ago, I passed the Detective Exam, so I'll stay here if the opportunity comes in the next six months or so; if not, I'll start looking elsewhere for a detective position. Despite what you might think of Emporia by now, my wife and I love the area."

Vernon was anxious to get on the subject, "As I mentioned on the phone, Luke, I am here unofficially to see if I can help Grimsley and the Anderson family figure out what's going on. All we know for sure is that Lincoln had nothing to do with this girl's death, and for some reason, the police never looked for any other suspects. I know you are not involved either from the arresting or investigating standpoint, but anything you can give us as background or any scuttlebutt around the station would be appreciated and treated confidentially."

"That's fine. I'm not sure I can help much, but by way of background, there is a fine line sometimes between the city and county police. The city mostly enforces the laws, traffic violations, car accidents, domestics, break-ins, and stuff like that. But for major crimes that need investigation, the county takes them. The crossover comes, perhaps like this situation, when the city police catch someone committing a major crime like armed robbery or murder. We make the arrest and schedule an arraignment hearing, and if the case moves forward, it gets referred to the county.

"Looking at the Hennessey girl, had Lincoln Anderson been standing over her with a gun, or his car was sitting on top of her, it might have been obvious he was guilty, and our guys would have arrested and tried to close the case. That's what they did here but without any obvious evidence. Clear?"

"Crystal," Vernon replied, "Any clue as to why, though?"

"You are now entering the scuttlebutt area and I do not mind speculating a bit, even though you need to understand that I have nothing to substantiate what I am about to say. First, the arresting officer Jerry Abbott is a piece of shit racist, sorry for the French. He gets called to the scene and finds a young Black kid over a white girl's body.

"That alone might have triggered a nuisance arrest, put the kid through the mill for no reason other than to piss off him and the Black Community. "Let them know we are tough on crime. But let's also imagine that Abbott knew who hit the kid, and it was one of his guys. Now, he wants to protect his buddy and, conveniently, can nail a Black kid at the same time. Following?"

"Sweet Jesus," James chimed in. "That might explain why they offered such a sweet deal to Lincoln with no jail time, but the offer came from Chief Dukes, not Abbott."

"Good observation, James," Blackwell continued, "the Chief is an enigma. My experience with him has been OK, but others, not so good. Again, my spin is that one of two things can be in play here. The first is the Chief's ego; he looks good if he can close this case quickly and without County involvement. The second is that some believe that the Chief and Abbott are mates, and if Abbott pushed Dukes, with or without explaining the details, Dukes might have gone along with it."

Vernon sat back, looked at James, then his watch, and said, "This is very helpful, Luke. We are meeting with Vanessa Walker after this and hopefully will learn the county's intentions. Should you hear anything, I would appreciate a call, and again, I can't thank you enough." Vern started to clear his trash and stood, offering his hand to Blackwell.

James added his gratitude and handshake, and they all walked out together.

Chapter 42

June 30th, Emporia

In James's car, Vernon said, "We got an hour to kill before we meet with Vanessa Walker; why not head back to the hotel and grab a quick bite?"

"Sounds good." James went back via I-95 as it was the quicker route, and it went around town in case the hooded crowd was still occupying downtown. Ten minutes later, they pulled in and went to their respective rooms. They reconvened in the hotel lobby at twelve-ten and realized the Courtyard did not have lunch. They settled for yogurt, peanut butter crackers, and bottles of water.

"I liked Luke Blackwell. Seems like a good guy," offered Brown.

"I agree! And his theory sounds good, but I don't know how we'll prove anything."

"We'll have to see what the county gal has to say. You ready?"

"Yep."

Ten minutes later, James and Vernon were parking at the County Court House, and there was no evidence of the morning's parade. They parked and entered the old, drab building. After they confirmed their appointment with Ms. Walker to the Security Guard, they went through electronic security and a quick wand frisk.

The directory next to the elevator showed that the County Commissioner, County Attorney, and Assistant County Attorney Vanessa Walker's officers were all on the third floor. They were greeted by a thirtyish, professionally dressed Black woman off the elevator behind a rich mahogany oval desk. This floor was a huge upgrade from the first-floor police station decor.

It was a moderately lavish office suite for three government officials with leather chairs and tasteful artwork. It boasted ample natural light from a large window overlooking Main Street. A coffee station was off in the corner.

The receptionist asked, "Good afternoon, gentlemen. May I help you?"

Vernon replied, "I'm sure you can; we have an appointment with Ms. Walker, James McNeil and Vernon Brown."

She confirmed with someone and said, "Right this way, please," and led them to a small conference room. "Ms. Walker will be in shortly. May I get you anything, coffee, tea, or water?"

Vernon and James looked at each other, and Vernon turned back to her, "Nothing for me, thank you."

"Me neither, thanks," James added.

The conference room continued the design theme of the lobby, a large rectangular mahogany table with eight leather armchairs. Several pieces of Civil War art and a painting of this very courthouse adorned the walls.

A light knock on the door was then promptly opened by a Black woman with a cocoa-hued skin tone and jet-black hair in a bob cut. The five-foot-six-inch woman had on a dark blue woman's business suit with a white blouse, pearl necklace, earrings, and bright red lipstick.

"Good afternoon, gentlemen, I'm Vanessa Walker," offering a smile and a handshake. The men stood, and Vernon returned the handshake, "I'm Detective Vernon Brown of the Philadelphia PD. We spoke on the phone yesterday. And this is James McNeil, my good friend, and the uncle of Lincoln Anderson." The handshakes concluded, and they all sat.

"Were you offered something to drink?"

"We were, and we're fine, thank you," Vernon replied.

Walker said, "I told you yesterday, detective, that I'm not certain how much I can share with you. We just got the case yesterday."

"I understand. James and I need to get back to Philly soon and want to do all we can to leave the Anderson family in good shape. If we could ask a few questions, anything you might be able to tell us, we would appreciate it. First, have you decided yet to proceed with the case against Lincoln?"

"No pussyfooting around, huh, detective. We have five days before the Preliminary Hearing, and we might use all five of those days to find out how we got here, what we do know, and what we don't."

James wanted to allow Vernon to lead on this, but he interjected, "Might you be able to tell us why the police never looked for any other suspects once Lincoln was falsely arrested?"

"That's begging the question, Mr. McNeil. We have not determined yet whether your nephew was falsely arrested. I do not know whom else the police may have considered, but I have detectives looking at that now."

Vernon asked, "Are you aware of the offer Chief Dukes made to Lincoln Anderson, a plea with no jail time if he would admit to involuntary manslaughter."

"I have read that but have not discussed it with the Chief. I can assure you I will."

"Is there anything else you can tell us that we have not told you?" Vernon asked, sensing the meeting was nearing its end.

"Yes! We will do the right thing for everyone in Emporia, including the Anderson and Hennessey families. We may not be able to do that in five days, but if the judge decides to continue with a trial, we'll have much more time to investigate. You're not recording me, are you? I have concerns about how this case was presented to the county; we will look at this very diligently. Are we good here?" She started to gather her papers and was clearly finished.

"I think we're good, Ms. Walker. We sincerely appreciate your seeing us and your candidness," Vernon Brown said while standing.

James stood also and added, "Yes, thanks so much, Ms. Walker."

They all shook hands and offered pleasantries. Walker showed them to the lobby.

Chapter 43

June 17th, Brookline

Well-satiated and still quiet after the tense lunch discussion, Detectives Duff and Flanagan sat in Duffy's car contemplating their next move.

Duffy took out his notebook and said to Flanagan, "There's still a couple of kids on our Top Ten list we have not talked to: Chip Waters, Byron Delgrasso, Noah Lancaster, and Jarrett Ashburn. Waters and Delgrasso were known drug users; perhaps we squeeze them to find out who they got their stuff from? It might have been Warren, but it could be someone else and potentially the Bossman. You have either of their addresses?"

Glad to finally be back on the subject, Kathy studied her smartphone and said, "Got them both, boss. Delgrasso is back in the Fisher Hill area, and Waters is up in Cottage Farm. Want me to call?"

"Nah! I prefer the element of surprise. Let's head out to Fisher Hill first and, if time allows, up to Cottage Farm."

Fisher Hill was out on the west end of Brookline, just east of Newton, the town known for its hills on the Boston Marathon route. Hyslop Road, where Delgrasso lived, was another affluent area with huge homes on large, tree-filled lots.

They pulled into the long drive, and there were five cars parked in the drive. Someone was obviously home; they hoped it was Byron. They parked and pulled out their badges, and Duffy rang the bell. An attractive forty-ish woman with a short blond bob haircut answered the door. "Hello, may I help you?"

"Yes, thank you. Might you be Mrs. Delgrasso? I am Detective Duffy, and this is my partner, Detective Flanagan, with the Brookline PD."

"I am Teresa Delgrasso; can I help you?"

"Yes, we'd like to speak with Byron if he's home."

"He is, but he's out back in the pool with a couple of friends. May I ask what this is in reference to?" She stepped back from the door, inviting them into the foyer.

Duffy replied, "Sure, we wanted to speak to him about Kelly Anderson's death at last week's graduation party."

"Byron is only a junior and was not at that party."

"Yes, we know that, Mrs. Delgrasso, but we are trying to talk to as many students as possible, searching for anything to help us find out how this happened. We will not keep him long. We would prefer to talk to him away from his friends. Might you ask him to come in or, come out front to speak to us?"

"Sure. We'll come out from the side of the house and meet you in the drive."

She left to retrieve her son, and Duffy and Flanagan walked out to the driveway.

A couple of minutes later, mother and son appeared, Byron with a towel drying off. Duffy made the introductions again and asked if they could speak alone with Byron. Mrs. Delgrasso hesitated but then walked back to the house.

Byron Delgrasso was about five foot nine and thin, perhaps even frail. He was dark-complected or tanned, with dark, wet hair. He had no tattoos or birthmarks, but he had a scar on his lower abdomen, extending down his bathing suit. Duffy thought it could be from the removal of his appendix.

Duffy said, "We'll only keep you a few minutes, Byron. We know you were not at the graduation party, but we have learned that you were suspected of using illegal drugs in the past. We are not here about that; we are anxious to know whom you obtained your stuff from."

Byron stared at Duffy but remained speechless. His body had tensed, and he cracked his knuckles. Sensing his concern, Kathy spoke up, "As Detective Duffy said, Byron, we are just looking for leads and are not here to discuss your personal drug situation. That's why we wanted to talk to you privately."

Seeming somewhat relieved, Byron finally said, "I got weed and Oxy from Shelly Warren, but I know nothing about who killed Shelly."

Duffy re-claimed the lead, "Did Shelly ever tell you who he got the stuff from?"

"Funny you should ask that. I once asked Shelly, and instead of saying, 'No one you know,' he said, 'I can't tell you that.' It made me think it was someone I must know."

"But you have no idea who that might be?"

"No, but at the time, I wondered if it might be some kid's dad, or someone at school, a teacher, or a janitor."

"One last question," Duffy said, "Who else in the school is offering drugs other than Shelly?"

"That's not an easy question, sir. I mean, a kid can buy from anyone. I have actually sold some of my supply to other kids, so how was I to know that Shelly was dealing or was selling me stuff from his personal stash? You know what I mean? But enough kids were getting it from Shelly that I was quite certain he was dealing. Do you think Shelly getting murdered is related to Kelly Reynolds's accidental death?"

"Only in the sense that they both involved drugs, Byron. Did you know if Shelly offered or had access to Roofies?"

"No, I never had a need for them."

Duffy ended this interview with, "This is good for now, Byron. Take my card and call me should you hear anything more; you can go back to your friends," handing him his card.

Back in the car, Flanagan said, "I think he knew more. Users know where to get their stuff, and I'd bet he's already learned who replaced Shelly Warren."

"I would not disagree with your read on that, Kath. Let's head up to Cottage Farm and try to catch this Waters kid."

Chapter 44

June 17th, Brookline

There was no easy way to get to the Cottage Farm area from where they were, and it took a good twenty-five minutes. Cottage Farm was in the northeast section of Brookline, about as far from Fisher Hill as you could get and remain in Brookline. It was just south of the Boston University campus. They found the Waters' residence on Worthington Road and, not to their surprise, another very large, expensive home.

"I guess we knew no poor kids went to this school despite all the scholarships they always advertise," Kathy said.

"Despite their best intentions, poor kids don't live in that area and have no peer group in the school. It's one of those white privilege things the sociologists and politicians talk about."

"Look at you get all philosophical."

Duffy parked the car, and they both approached the house. The front door was open, and they rang the bell. A fourteen-year-old girl came to the door and asked, "Yeah?"

Duffy replied, "We are looking for Chip Waters; are you his sister?"

"Yeah, but he's not home. Do you want my mom? Mom!" she yelled, not waiting for an answer.

Presumably, Mrs. Waters appeared and asked, "May I help you?"

Duffy showed his badge and replied, "Detectives Duffy and Flanagan, Mrs. Waters. We are hoping to speak with your son, Chip. Your daughter said he might not be home."

Mrs. Waters chose to step out of the house rather than invite them in. She said, "That's right, but he's only at the Amory Playground playing basketball, if this is important. Has he done something wrong, detective?"

"Not at all; we just wanted to speak to him about the death of Kelly Reynolds and now another student, Sheldon Warren."

"I'm not certain what he can tell you, but you can catch him there. You won't miss him; he's wearing a Larry Bird green Celtics jersey."

Duffy said, "Thanks, we'll give it a try."

The Amory Playground was a two-minute drive and had basketball and tennis courts, in addition to a kids' playground and picnic area with benches. A thick forest of trees outlined the property, and from within, you'd never know there were homes adjacent.

It wasn't difficult finding Chip Waters with the green jersey. He was playing three on three, half-court game, and Duffy and Flanagan walked directly to him, withdrawing their badges. Duffy said, "Chip Waters, I am Detective Duffy, and this is Detective Flanagan. We'd like to ask a few questions. Sorry to interrupt, guys; we'll only keep him a few minutes."

Play had come to a stop, and all eyes were on Duffy as he led Waters off the court and towards a bench. As they sat, Waters asked, "What's this about?"

Kathy answered, "It's about the deaths of Kelly Reynolds and Sheldon Warner."

Waters responded, "I didn't know Kelly at all and don't know anything about either of their deaths."

Duffy took over again as if on cue, "Nonetheless, we have a couple of questions for you. Did you get your drugs from Warner?"

Waters froze. His body stiffened, and he steepled his hands while he gathered himself. *Fess up or lie*, he thought to himself; *lie, of course, see what they got.* "What are you talking about? I don't have any drugs."

"You take us for fools, Chip? How do you think we got your name? If you would prefer, we can do this down the station with your mom and dad." Duffy wanted to remind the kid who was in charge; point taken.

"Yeah, OK, I occasionally got some stuff from Shelly, but I don't have any idea who killed him. I hadn't seen him since school ended.

And I told you, I did not know Kelly Reynolds at all, and I was not at the graduation party."

"If it helps, Chip, we don't think you were involved with either of their deaths; we are just looking for information," Duffy continued. "Did Shelly ever tell you who he got the stuff from?"

"He never mentioned a name, but something he said once made me think it might have been a teacher. Something like, 'He probably has a desk full of the stuff.'"

Kathy asked, "Do you recall what class you were in at the time?"

"I do; it was definitely science because I said something like he could be Brookline's Walter White, you know, like *Breaking Bad*."

"And the science teacher's name?"

"Mr. Newman, but I can't swear he's the guy. We were just in his room at the time."

"We understand, Chip, and we'll keep your name in confidence for the time being. I think we have enough for now. You can get back to your game. Thanks, Chip." Duffy was satisfied that he was not getting anything more from Waters, and they had a new name.

They got back into the car and headed back to the station. He had a text from Captain Price asking for an update.

Chapter 45

June 17th, Brookline

It always seemed like rush hour in the Greater Boston area, and at three-fifteen in the afternoon, Kent Street was stop-and-go, but it seemed more like stop.

Duffy asked, "Kent Street all the way in?" as if Kathy knew a shortcut that had been kept a secret from the rest of the world.

"I think so unless you think St. Paul would be better, but I'd stay the course, Duff."

"How about trying to call that Lassiter woman and find out what you can about that science teacher."

"Good idea!" Kathy looked through her phone and, finding Lassiter, placed the call to Lassiter's cell phone.

"Hello?" Lassiter answered.

"Hello, Colleen, this is Detective Kathy Flanagan, remember me? Might you have a minute?"

"Sure, Kathy; what can I do for you?"

"What can you tell me about a science teacher named Newman?"

"Jeff Newman? What might you want to know?"

"I'm not certain. His name came up in our investigation. Anything you can tell us, how long he's been there, his reputation, the good, bad and ugly."

"Nice guy, thirty-five years old, has been with us for about eight years, I would say. He's quite popular with the students and gets good reviews. There was a matter about two years ago, and Dr. Breckenridge had to speak with him. One of the female students complained he had made her feel uncomfortable. I think it was his use of some sexual innuendo. It might have been a misunderstanding, and I do not believe there have been other issues."

"Anything at all about drugs?"

"Oh no!" Lassiter offered and then hesitated. "Off the record, now that you ask, he occasionally looks a bit wiped out, just red eyes. But I know he has a young daughter, and possibly he was just sleep-deprived. I'm not an expert on that stuff."

"That's helpful, Colleen, I appreciate it. Enjoy the rest of your summer."

"You're welcome, Kathy; you too."

Kathy updated Duffy on the conversation as they pulled in and parked at the station.

Duffy and Flanagan went to their adjoining desks, but Captain Price had seen them enter and waved them into his office.

"I guess we need to go update him; let's go," Duffy said to his partner.

They entered Price's office, and he directed them to sit. "What do you have, something I hope?" Price was looking at Duffy, expecting he would be the one to answer.

"Been a long day, Cap. We went to tell Tyler Longenecker about his friend's death, and he admitted that he occasionally got some stuff from Warren. I suspect it was more than occasionally. We then went to see two kids known to be drug users, and both also mentioned Warren. But the one kid also mentioned that Warren had once let it slip that a science teacher named Jeff Newman could be involved in some way, possibly as Warren's supplier. We need to contact him tomorrow."

Price said, "For my benefit primarily, let me see if I can summarize. We know that someone gave the Reynolds girl a roofie and then raped her. No one knows for sure who that might be, but the Tyler kid was the last kid to be seen with her.

"So far, the only drug connection seems to be this Warren kid, who's known to distribute. Then he gets killed, presumably by his supplier, who needs to eliminate the connection. We have two murders, and even if Warren's supplier is the one who killed him, that does not get us much closer to who killed Reynolds. Have I got this right?"

Duffy looked to Flanagan and then back to Price. "That's about it, Cap. Anything else, Kath?"

"Only that we hope if we can nail the supplier, we can find out who got the roofies, but there is no guarantee the supplier would know that."

Price asked, "Anyone else on that Top Ten list of yours to interview?"

Duffy replied, "Not really; I still believe the answer is with that mystery girl who originally reported the Reynolds girl. I think we might need to interview every girl again, but I don't quite understand her reluctance to step up. If she was culpable, why report it at all?"

Kathy answered, "It's possible she was concerned that Reynolds needed some medical attention but just didn't want to be implicated or rat out a kid."

Price had heard enough and said, "So, you'll pursue this teacher and then re-interview all the girls at the party. We could use a break. The Chief is on my ass every day. Thanks, guys."

Duffy and Flanagan stood and took a step towards the door. Just then, Price said, "Kathy, can you hold back a minute?"

Duffy and Flanagan both stopped. Duffy looked at Kathy, then turned and walked out, closing the door behind him.

Kathy turned to the captain but remained standing. She bit her lip and waited.

"You coming to the apartment tonight? I thought we'd order in Chinese."

"I don't think so, Hank."

"What's up?"

"I think we should resume a professional relationship. I am uncomfortable with this arrangement and think it's best to end it before it gets too deep."

"It's deep already, Kathy. Did something happen?"

"Duffy knows!"

"Did you tell him?"

"No, he figured it out the other night when he called us both at midnight and heard the same TV show in the background. But I had had concerns before that. You're married, and you're my boss. We both know better, Hank. It won't end good and will get worse the longer it goes on. Please respect my wishes, and let's try to move on."

She looked at him for a response and turned to leave when he said, "I'm not sure I can do that, Kathy."

She walked out, wondering to herself what he meant by that.

Fortunately, Duffy had left by the time she returned to her desk.

Chapter 46

June 30th, Emporia

After they met with Vanessa Walker, Vernon Brown called Grimsley's office to see if Lincoln's attorney was available for a quick update. His assistant said he could be available at two-thirty. It was one-forty-five, so Vernon and James decided to have a cup of coffee at a cafe on Main Street before walking across the street to Grimsley's.

It had been an hour since they last ate, so they decided to share an apple fritter with their coffee. The cute little cafe had no table service; you ordered and picked up at the counter. There were five small tables and a six-foot counter with four stools facing out onto Main Street. You could also buy tee shirts and mugs if you chose to advertise the cafe.

"What are we going to tell Grimsley?" James asked his crime-fighting mentor.

"We'll bring him up-to-date on our meetings with Blackwell and Walker. It's still tough to draw any conclusions, but I think our focus should be on why the Chief wanted to get rid of the case so quickly. He or someone might be covering up for someone, and that would mean a friend, family, or officer him or herself. Agree?"

"But why arrest Lincoln?"

"I don't think it was racial initially. I think they were waiting for the first person to stop. When it turned out to be a Black kid, so much the better for Abbott and the Chief."

"I like your thinking, Vern. Let's plan to wrap it up tomorrow and head home on Thursday. I think we've done enough, and truth be told, I'm not certain Walker wants to pursue the case against Lincoln."

"I'm good. Let's beat the holiday weekend traffic."

At two-twenty-five, they walked across the street and up to Grimsley's office. Grimsley's assistant greeted them expectantly and took them right to his office. Grimsley came out from behind his desk, greeted them, and suggested they sit at the coffee table. Drinks were declined.

Grimsley said, "Anything new to report, gentlemen?"

James deferred again to Vernon, who replied, "We met this morning with Luke Blackwell and this afternoon with Vanessa Walker. There was a common theme as both suggested that the attempt by Chief Dukes to squelch any investigation is telling, even though neither could be quite certain of what. Collective speculation is to cover up for someone, either a friend or family member or one of the officers. But there is no obvious suspect. Walker was extremely coy when asked if she would pursue the case, saying they had just started their investigation."

"Everything is going to script, I would say. While I would love to find the doer if there is one, we can win this case at trial. But I honestly do not believe Vanessa wants to take this to trial. I think she is looking for a way to dismiss without embarrassing the Emporia PD or the Chief."

"Glad to hear you say that, Malcolm. James and I are thinking of wrapping things up tomorrow and going home on Thursday. It would be great if we could ID the suspect, but we are not even certain there is one. Hopefully, we have been somewhat helpful to you and the Andersons, but unless something comes up tomorrow, I think we are done. I'd like to take a run at Chief Dukes. You think he would meet with us?"

"He just might, now that the case is with the County, and the Chief would like to appear to be taking the high road. I'll call him and text you."

James added, "That would be great, Malcolm, and again, I want to thank you for allowing us to participate down here. I know this is a bit unusual."

"You're welcome, and I appreciate your assistance. But you're not done with me yet; I'll see you at dinner."

"That'll be great; see you then." James and Vernon stood, shook hands, and left Grimsley's office.

"You ready to leave James," Vernon asked his friend.

"I will be on Thursday for sure. I do hope we can speak with Dukes tomorrow, just for some closure."

"I'm not quite certain what to ask him or what answers we might expect. We'll play deferential to him and stroke his ego a bit. He might be more forthcoming if he thinks we respect him."

"Got it! Four o'clock, and we just time to call home, shower, and take a short nap. Leave at five-thirty? Give us time to pick a bottle or two of wine, perhaps some flowers."

"I'll be there," Vern replied.

They parked and went to their rooms. When Vernon got to him, the red MESSAGE WAITING light was flashing on the room's phone. *Who could that be*, Vernon wondered. *Everyone I know has my cell number.* He called to get the message, "Hello, Detective Brown. This is Clark Kent. I'd like to meet with you tomorrow, any time, any place. I have information relevant to your case." He left his cell number. *More intrigue, and I'm Lex Luther.*

Vernon wasn't sure if he should use his cell phone. Clark Kent did not have that number. He decided it wasn't much of a risk and dialed the number Kent had left.

"Hello?"

"Hello, is this Clark Kent?"

"It is; thanks for returning my call, Detective Brown. As I said in my message, I'd like to meet with you tomorrow. Is there a good time?"

"You want me to come to a meeting with Clark Kent with no further explanation?"

"I would; I don't want to give it on the phone, but I'll give it to you in person when I see you. As I said, I think it is important and will help your case."

"I'm curious, but I'm unsure of the timing just yet. I am waiting to hear if I have a meeting with Chief Dukes, but don't know the time. How about I text you later? Oh, I'll have my friend with me."

"That'll be fine, I'll look forward to meeting Mr. McNeil also. I'll text you the location. Thanks, detective." They both hung up.

Now, what the hell is this about? Vernon thought to himself.

He continued thinking about it as he showered, called Ronnie, and failed at trying to take a nap. He hadn't carried his gun since they had been here but felt safer carrying it tonight.

He met James at precisely five-thirty in the hotel lobby. "I've got a story for you, but you'll have to wait until I tell everyone at dinner," Vernon teased.

They made a quick stop at the nearby liquor store and picked up one red and one white wine. They did not see a place to buy flowers. They pulled up at the Andersons at five to six. All of the Andersons were present, as well as Malcolm Grimsley and his wife Beatrice. Hugs, handshakes, and drinks were the first order. The tantalizing smell of fried chicken filled the house.

At six-forty, Estelle called them into the dining room set for nine. The food was all on the table, and mashed potatoes, gravy, collard greens, cranberries, and homemade biscuits joined the chicken. Dwight suggested grace, and they all held hands.

Vernon Brown couldn't wait much longer, "Before we all fill our mouths, I have an interesting update. When we got back to the hotel, I had a voicemail message waiting, and it turned out to be from Clark Kent. He would not tell me his real name until I agreed to meet with him tomorrow. He did say he had something important to the case to tell me. How about them apples?"

They all looked around the table at each other, wondering who would start the question-and-answer discussion. "Whoa! This is huge," James started. "He gave you no hint?"

"None at all."

Grimsley said, "Interesting indeed, but I'd be careful. If someone thinks you're getting too close, this could be dangerous, Vernon."

Estelle, not wanting her hard work to get cold, said, "Let's eat; we can discuss as we eat." She picked up and passed the chicken platter around. The filling of plates, eating, and further discussion lasted forty-five minutes.

Lincoln Anderson said, "I've got news; I had a call today from Coach Blackwell. He was just checking in and looking for an update. I thought that was nice of him."

"It was, James said, "He knows which side of his toast is buttered. He wants to make certain his MVP shows up in September."

When it appeared everyone was finished eating, Estelle stood and said, "Why don't y'all go into the living room and let us clean-up for dessert?" They all stood at once, and Lincoln, Tawana, and Neek stayed to help their mom clean up. They had a system; Estelle put away the leftovers, Tawana rinsed them, and passed them to Neek, who loaded the dishwasher. After Lincoln cleared the table, he set out coffee cups, dessert plates, and forks.

When the clean-up ended, Estelle brought out Pecan and Key Lime pies and a half gallon of vanilla ice cream and summoned the crowd to the table.

"Oh my," Beatrice Grimsley exclaimed. "How do you get the time to do all this?"

"I love to cook and don't get the chance to cook for so many friends; dig in."

Estelle cut the pies, took orders, instructed Tawana to pour coffee, and asked Dwight to add the ice cream to the Pecan Pie. Lots of oohs and aahs as the desserts were tasted.

By eight-fifteen, the dessert plates had been removed, and all were ready to call it a night. As they gathered in the living room, Grimsley said, "Bea and I are hoping we can take y'all out tomorrow night for a final meal. We made a reservation at Miss Sabrina's up the road."

Vernon said, "That is very nice of you, Malcolm. I'm not certain I'll be ready to eat again by then, but if so, I think you count James and me in."

Estelle answered, "You can count on Dwight and me, but we'll leave the kids home with pizza. Thank you, Bea and Malcolm."

"Reservation is at six-thirty. Vernon, if anything comes up in your meeting with Superman tomorrow, please call me on my cell. Good luck and be careful."

"Will do!"

They all thanked Estelle and Dwight again and returned to their cars.

Chapter 47

June 18th, Brookline

It was going to be a hot summer day, near ninety. It was partly cloudy, and thundershowers were predicted.

Duffy and Flanagan had agreed that talking to this Jeff Newman was their priority, and Duffy picked up Kathy at eight-thirty. Colleen Lassiter had provided them with Newman's address down in Dorchester. Duffy had picked up two coffees on his way, and Kathy was appreciative.

"What's up this morning, Duff?"

"Not much, another Red Sox loss; how about with you?"

"You'll be glad to know that I broke it off with Price yesterday."

"Was that why he asked you to stay after our meeting?"

"No, he wanted me to go over last night; that's when I chose to end it."

"I hope you did not do it because of me; no one takes my advice seriously."

"Not entirely, Duff, but after we talked, it made me feel dirty. I didn't like the feeling. So, I'm appreciative of your advice."

"And was he OK with it?"

"Not exactly, but he'll find a replacement quickly, I hope. Guys like him have a list of women to pursue."

They pulled into the Newman driveway at nine-fifteen and approached the front door of the modest colonial brick house. The door was open, and Kathy rang the bell. A rather plain woman in her mid-thirties rushed to the door, being trailed by a three-year-old little girl. It appeared to both that the woman was or had been crying.

"Hello?" was all she could get out.

"Mrs. Newman? We are Detectives Flanagan and Duffy from Brookline. Is your husband available?"

"Come in; I'm Taylor Newman, but I'm afraid I don't know where my husband is."

She led them into the small living room off the foyer. The daughter was now clinging to her mother, wary of the strangers. "I thought perhaps you were here to tell me he'd been in an accident."

"No, when was the last you saw him?" Kathy continued.

"Tuesday morning. He came home late that night and left early yesterday morning. He left me a note that he was going to the gym and breakfast with his friend, Harvey. He has not answered his phone or responded to text messages. When he had not returned by four, I called Harvey, who had not seen or heard from him yesterday. I called a few of his friends and brother, but no one had spoken to him. This has never happened before; I'm scared to death."

"You have not called the local police yet?" Duffy asked.

"No, Harvey said he'd be over at about nine, and we could discuss what to do."

"Has your husband mentioned any problems, or has he been acting differently?" Kathy asked.

"Like everyone at school, I think, the deaths of that young girl and the Warren kid upset him. He's a pretty private guy; I think he keeps a lot to himself."

Kathy said, "What is his cell number, and what kind of car is your husband driving?"

"A white Nissan SUV," she said as she gave him the cell number. She stepped outside and called the station to put a trace on the cell phone. She returned to the living room.

Kathy added, "I've asked our staff to track his phone. That will take a little time. Since your friend is coming over to stay with you, we'll take off to lead the search. Please call us should you hear anything, and we'll give you an update later this morning. OK?"

"I guess so. I appreciate whatever you can do."

They stood, and Kathy smiled at the little girl as if it might help, but she feared the worst.

Chapter 48

June 18th, Brookline

"Whatta you thinking, Kathy?"

"I think the same as you, Duff; nothing good has happened to Mr. Newman. The question might be, just how not good?"

"But it does suggest that he might be the supplier. He never killed anyone before, found himself needing to kill Warren, and now is struggling not only with murder but the fact we may be on to him for the drugs."

"May I ask where we are going? You keeping a secret?"

"Wise ass! No sense heading back to the station, so I thought we'd go midway between his home, the school, and the station. I'm sure you told someone how urgent this was."

"Of course! There's a Whole Foods with a Starbucks on Perkins Road, should you need a second cup."

"That's as good as I'd come up with."

Fifteen minutes later, they sat in Starbucks with their coffee. Trying to make conversation, Kathy asked, "Duff, tell me, how do you and Cindy do it? I mean, how does she tolerate a cop's life?"

"Thanks for the softball question. Cindy's dad was a cop, and her sister is a cop. I think that helps. They understand the pressure, the hours, even the stress. But even with all of that, it's not easy. We went to counseling for a year after my second son, Michael, was born. Her understanding is critical, but my remembering my role as her husband is even more important. Uh, who's pitching for the Sox tonight?"

Kathy smiled and said, "The witness may step down."

Five minutes later, her cell rang, "Flanagan," she answered.

"Thanks, Alex. Would you alert Captain Price and send an ambulance out there, please? I fear we may need one, or maybe I hope we need one." She said to Duffy, "They got a ping on the cellphone at the *Allerton Overlook*; let's go."

They put lids on their half-full coffees and scooted to the car. *Olmstead Park* was a fifteen-acre area close to *Virginia's*, where they ate lunch yesterday. The Overlook was on Pond Avenue on the west side of the Leverett Pond that occupied half of the park.

With the siren on, they got there in eight minutes and picked up Pond Avenue off of Chestnut Street. As they approached the parking area, they slowed down to a crawl. "Shit!" Duffy exclaimed, "I never saw so many white SUVs."

But five minutes later, Duffy slowed down again so Kathy could check the license plate. "Got it," she exclaimed. I don't see anyone in it; I'll check."

Duffy turned the car off and stretched while Kathy approached the SUV. She peered in the passenger side window and turned to Duffy with an extended thumb down. Duffy was not certain if that meant no one was there or someone was there and not doing well. Kathy tried the door but found it locked. She waved to Duffy to come over. The two stared at a man's body slumped over the console towards the passenger's seat.

"Did either of us think of asking Mrs. Newman for their car fob?" Duffy asked rhetorically. "Call the station, cancel the ambulance, and ask for the CSI team."

Duffy returned to his car and returned with a tire iron. It took three swings for the window to shatter and spray glass onto the street, the inside of the car, and onto Jeff Newman. Duffy reached in, opened the door, and felt for a nonexistent pulse.

"And then there were three," Duffy mumbled to no one in particular.

They looked in and around the car, finding an empty container of Ritalin and a quarter-filled bottle of Old Forester. It seemed obvious this was a suicide, but they would let the forensic team make that call.

In the car trunk, they found a backpack half-filled with assorted pills, weed, and white powders. Duffy believed they had their dealer. *It went from Newman to Warren, now both deceased, but then to whom?* Duffy speculated to himself.

When the forensic team arrived, Duffy and Kathy returned to the station. Duffy left a message for Captain Price. They stopped by his office, and he waved them to sit down. "What did you learn?" Price asked.

Duffy replied, "Only that it appears to be a suicide and that Newman was the source of the drugs. He would have supplied the Warren kid, but still no clue as to who he may have given or sold the roofies to."

"Any possibility that Warren himself was the doer?"

Duffy responded, "There is no evidence to that, but it remains a possibility. I don't think anyone would be satisfied if we claim the case was closed and Warren was the killer."

"Next step?"

"There's nothing to do except keep drilling down on these kids, hoping someone will crack. We know that the girl who alerted the server and the doer himself are at least two who know. Finding the girl would be more likely. Any suggestions, Cap?" Duffy asked.

"Not really but keep me posted."

Duffy and Flanagan left Price's office, and Duffy couldn't help but notice Kathy and Price avoided eye contact. *None of my business*, he thought.

Chapter 49

July 1ˢᵗ, Emporia

By the time Vernon and James returned to the hotel last night, Brown had heard from Grimsley that Chief Dukes could meet with them at three o'clock today. He texted his availability to Clark Kent, who said eleven o'clock at a Dairy Queen about twenty miles east of Emporia.

After a late breakfast at Cracker Barrel, they both made calls to their wives, and Brown checked in with his partner, Roberta Brumson. Nothing demanded his attention. At ten-thirty, they were on Route 58, heading to the DQ. James and Vernon speculated about this mystery, but neither had a clue.

They arrived at five of eleven. James parked, and they looked around. There was only a half dozen cars in the parking lot at this hour. It appeared the DQ had just opened, and three people were in line: two teenage boys and a middle-aged white woman. They saw no one in a red cape or Clark Kent glasses, so they parked and stepped up to the window.

As they waited, a tall, lean, white man approached them. Dressed casually in a VCU tee-shirt and shorts, he stepped up to them and said, "Vernon Brown? I'm Clark Kent, and you must be James McNeil," he said confidently, extending his hand to both.

"So, the dance continues," Brown responded.

"I'll clear that up shortly; let's go inside; there are tables we can sit at. Dessert is on me."

James said, "I don't pass up DQ, Mr. Kent, so I'll take you up on your generous offer." James ordered a small M&M Blizzard, and the others did the same. They returned to a table in the corner. No one else was sitting, and Mr. Kent felt comfortable with their privacy.

"Sorry about all of the intrigue, but I think you'll understand after I tell you. My name is Steve Greenfield, or should I say, Special Agent Greenfield, with the FBI?" He removed his badge and handed it to Vernon.

Satisfied, Vernon returned it to Greenfield, "That's a relief. I can put the safety back on my Glock."

"I'm undercover in the KKK. The FBI's Richmond office has me and two other agents in Virginia and South Carolina hate groups. I was in the parade in Emporia the other day. Fun people to party with," Greenfield said with his tongue in cheek.

"Just what is it you do?" Brown asked.

"It's not illegal to belong to these groups, but we monitor their activities. We're not concerned with parades and demonstrations, but we want to be alert to any potential violence. That cross-burning at your family's the other night, James, was at the last minute and was conducted by two or three members. I did not know about it in advance."

Vernon said, "You said you had something that might help James' nephew?"

Greenfield took out his cell phone and opened the pictures. He handed it to Vernon while saying, "This is the police vehicle that hit the Hennessey girl. Flip to the next picture, which is the bumper of the vehicle showing a small scratch where it struck her bike. It may have been fixed, but it's so small, I doubt it."

James asked the obvious, "How you'd get these?"

"If I told you that, I'd have to kill you, James. But if you get these pictures to Vanessa Walker, she can determine who had that vehicle at the time of the accident. On TV, I think they call this the *Smoking Gun*."

Vernon asked, "Do you have a theory on this, Steve?"

"I do, but it's only a theory. The officer hit the kid; he or she may have been drinking, tired, or just daydreaming. Probably checked and saw she was dead. Scared to come forward, waited for someone else to discover her body and arrested the Anderson kid. It's also possible the officer told Chief Dukes, and thus the cover-up began."

"This is fantastic, Steve," James said, "I can't thank you enough."

"No need, but I have one other tidbit you might want to pass on to Grimsley and your family. Officer Jerry Abbott is a card-carrying KKK member. I'd be wary of him; to say he's not a nice guy would be redundant."

"That might explain a lot."

"I'll text you these pictures, Vernon; I trust you can get them to Walker. These should get your nephew in the clear, James, so my work is done here, Lois! Might I ask one favor, please do not give my name to anyone, including your family. Just tell them you met with Clark Kent, and he refused to give his true identity.

"Good to meet you both; have a safe trip back to Philly."

They all stood, shook hands, and parted ways.

James and Vernon looked forward to meeting with the Chief and dinner tonight with the family.

Chapter 50

July 1st, Emporia

With several hours to kill before they met with Chief Dukes, James and Vernon thought they should do some shopping for their wives. They returned to downtown Emporia and parked. Vernon said he noticed a couple of shops on Main Street. Neither were great shoppers, but after thirty minutes had found earrings/necklace sets and some gag gifts of coffee mugs and spice sets to remember their trip to Emporia. The clerk was kind enough to wrap the jewelry.

They returned to the hotel; neither was hungry, and they expected another big meal night. They agreed to meet in the lobby at two-forty-five. Vernon placed a call to Vanessa Walker's office. "Ms. Walker's office," her assistant answered.

"This is Detective Brown from Philadelphia; we met with Ms. Walker yesterday. Is she available, please?"

"She is in court right now. May I help with something?"

"I have something very important to send her, so all I need is her cell number or email address."

"I cannot give out her cell number, but here is her email address: VWalkerACA@GreensburgCounty.gov."

"That's perfect, thanks so much."

Vernon sent off the pictures with a brief "I'm sure you'll find these helpful" note.

At five to three, Vernon and James were once again parked behind the courthouse and made their way to Chief Dukes' office. They offered seats, and both fiddled with their cell phones for ten minutes before the chief opened the door and summoned them in. Dukes was polite but in no way welcoming.

"What can I do for you?" Dukes asked curtly.

James had suggested that Vernon would do the talking.

Vernon replied, "Thanks for meeting with us, chief. We are heading back to Philly in the morning and hope you might answer a couple of remaining questions."

"Anything that would not jeopardize the investigation or the trial."

"Fair enough; do you still think Lincoln is guilty of something?"

"Not for me to say anymore, but yes, I do."

"Anything you would do differently if this happened tomorrow?"

"I might have referred it to the County immediately, but at the time, it looked like we could close the case quickly."

"And with no evidence, why did you not look for other suspects?"

"I'm not going to comment on the evidence, but searching for anyone else would have been a waste of our time."

"Thanks for your time, chief," as James and Vernon stood to leave. Vernon couldn't resist adding, "Chief, I don't know what's going on here, but you will regret the day you arrested Lincoln Anderson. Good day!"

Vernon and James left his office and the building.

"Nicely done, brother; you said just enough."

Chapter 51

June 19th, Hilton Head

At seven-thirty in the morning, I am sitting on my deck overlooking the Broad Creek on Hilton Head. I was enjoying my second cup of coffee while reading the *Philadelphia Inquirer* on my iPad. It was already eighty-two degrees with eighty-five percent humidity. When it got any hotter, I'd retreat to the air conditioning. With thundershowers predicted, I did not have golf plans.

My cell phone buzzed; it was Coach O from Duke. "Patrick, it's a beautiful day on Hilton Head. How are you, my friend?"

"Well, it's a shitty day in Durham, Goldy, I need to see you today?"

"Are you on the Island?"

"No, are you paying attention? I'm in Durham."

"You'd like me to drive somewhere? Like where?"

"I was thinking Fayetteville?"

"And I was thinking Bluffton, so how about we make it Florence? There's a *Buffalo Wild Wings* off the I-95 Exit. I'll need about three and a half hours to get there."

"I might need four; see you there, Goldy, thanks."

It was obvious the Coach did not want to offer details on the phone, but it was also very clear he considered this urgent. I jumped in the shower, threw on a Villanova tee shirt to infuriate Coach, refilled my coffee, and toasted a bagel for the road.

Why was I hurrying? Florence was closer for me than him. I decided I would get the car washed and filled with gas, and head for Florence. I was obsessed about being at least ten minutes early. And I would need to make an estimated two pee stops.

At eleven-thirty, I was twenty miles from my Florence exit. I made my final pit stop and called Coach for a travel update. "I'm just approaching Lumberton, forty to forty-five minutes to Florence."

"That's good. I'll beat you, and I'll go in, get a booth, and order us some wings. Still doing medium-hot Buffalo?"

"That'll be fine, Goldy."

"Take your time, brother."

I pulled into the *Buffalo Wild Wings* at exactly noon. The lot was less than half full. I got us a booth and ordered wings: half medium hot Buffalo and the other half garlic parmesan. I would allow myself one beer but told the server I would wait to order it. I played with my phone and did *Wordle and Connections* to share with my granddaughters.

Twenty minutes later, Coach Patrick O'Shea of Duke University walked towards me. I stepped out of the booth to greet him with a hug, "Great to see you, Coach. OK drive down?"

"No complaint. Thanks again, Goldy, for meeting me; you won't believe this shit."

"Sit down, relax, we'll order a couple of beers. I'm sure the wings will be out shortly."

O'Shea sat, and the server magically appeared. We both ordered Michelob Ultra drafts.

Finally, I said, "Take a deep breath! Let it out slowly. Now, what's going on?"

Somewhat relaxed, the Coach handed me his phone, saying, "I got this video anonymously last night. Just press play."

I did; I watched a teenage boy and girl, each holding a bottle of something, walk into what appeared to be a tent or a pool cabana. It appears the video stops. When it resumes, three other boys enter the cabana. There is another pause in the video. It resumes, but this time, the view is inside with the four boys staring at the girl lying on a settee, appearing asleep.

There is no audio. I suspect they are asking what they should do. But then, all four of them are undressing the girl. *Oh no,* I say to myself, feeling that I should be doing something. But I can't! The video resumes: the boys seem to be talking, and then one kid takes off his trousers and underwear. He leans over the girl; his next move is obvious. I stopped it and handed the phone back to the Coach.

We stared at each other, the Coach waiting for my flippant comment. *Sorry, Coach, not today.*

The server delivered the wings. Neither Coach nor I looked at her or the wings.

I finally asked, "What the hell is this, Pat?"

"You don't know? Do you recognize anyone?"

"No! Should I?"

"Yes, you should. The kid who took the girl in and had sex with her is none other than Tyler Longenecker."

"You're shitting me."

"I wish I were, Goldy, I wish I were."

"Um...who have you shown this, and a better question, why me?"

"No one, Goldy. I don't want to ruin the kid's life if this is a fraud or a sick joke. I value your opinion."

"Thanks, Patrick, but you'll have to allow the police to determine the authenticity. Do you know if this incident is out in public?"

"Are you kidding? The girl died, and there is a huge ongoing investigation. A reporter from Boston sent me the story when it first happened, not suspecting Longenecker was involved."

"I'm sorry about that, Pat, I really am, but you have no options. It's possible whoever sent this to you sent it to the police also, but you can't sit on this. Make your AD aware of it also."

"Before you rank prospects, do you investigate their character?"

"We're not muckrakers, Coach. If we learn about anything public, it may affect our ranking, and we might add that in a summary, but we do not investigate on our own. My very vague recollection is that my son-in-law had some doubts about the kid, and that was why we did not rank him a bit higher. So other than that, Mrs. Lincoln, how did you enjoy the play?"

"There's that perverse sense of humor I love so much."

"Look, this sucks for the poor girl's family and Tyler's family, but let me tell you, you are better off without this kid. At some point, his character would have surfaced and been an issue for you, Coach."

"I guess you're right."

"You have enough to eat, or you want to share a sandwich?"

"I'm good; I'll probably have indigestion as it is."

Coach O waved to the server for the check, settled it, and we made for the door. In the lot, we waved, and I said, "Let me know what happens, will you? And have a safe ride back."

"Thanks again, Goldy. Next month, I'll come down for a couple of days, and we'll play a bit of golf."

We parted, and all I could think of was *Holy Shit*!

Chapter 52

July 1st, Emporia

After leaving Chief Dukes, Vernon and James returned to the hotel. They decided not to update anyone except their wives on the day's meetings. They would do that at dinner and make it a very pleasant evening.

In their respective rooms, they both were doing the same things: calling wives, packing for tomorrow's departure, napping, and showering. They met in the lobby at six-fifteen for the short trip to Miss Sabrina's.

As instructed, they took Main Street to Route 301 and went North for three miles. Miss Sabrina's occupied a lot of its own, and they pulled onto the gravel parking lot. The lot was three-quarters filled. The red brick building was old but well maintained with freshly painted, dark green shutters and front door. The grass border surrounding the building was recently mowed, and the flower beds were in full bloom.

"And you thought Emporia was the fast-food capital of the South," James said to Vernon.

"It would take more than this one cute restaurant to change my mind, but I'm impressed so far."

They entered the restaurant and the small foyer area with six chairs. Two young women were standing behind a rostrum, selecting a table for the couple in front of them. They looked around and saw a pleasant and sparkling clean dining room and a second, smaller room off to the left. Red tablecloths and black napkins were on the tables; white lace curtains covered the windows, and shades had been pulled down to block out the sun.

One of the women took the couple to a table, and James stepped up and said, "We are meeting the Grimsleys."

"Oh yes, they are all here. Just a moment, and Priscilla will show you to the table." Priscilla promptly returned and was told to show us to the Grimsley table. We followed her through the large dining room to the second, smaller one, and there they were, all sitting at a table in the corner. James thanked Priscilla for the escort.

The Grimsleys and Andersons all stood to greet them with hugs and handshakes. "No trouble finding the place?" Malcolm Grimsley asked.

James replied, "None at all; it's hard to get lost in Emporia. Y'all been waiting long? We were five minutes early."

"We were ten," replied Dwight.

Vernon added, "A very nice place; I take back everything I said about dining in Emporia."

A server with a name tag came up to the table and said, "Good evening, my name is Millie, and I am looking forward to serving you tonight. May I bring anyone a drink?"

Malcolm responded, "I suspect you may bring everyone a drink, ladies?"

Everyone ordered a drink, and Millie left.

Estelle said, "You gonna keep us waiting, James? Tell us about your big meetings today."

"These are good stories, Estelle, and I don't want to be interrupted when Millie returns, so let's wait for the drinks. What did y'all do today?"

"It won't take long to tell you what Dwight and I did; we spent two hours in Walmart, and that was our day. Sorry, I did a bit of baking, a loaf of bread, and a Pecan Pie to replace the one y'all ate last night," she smiled.

Malcolm Grimsley said, "I filed a motion to dismiss the case against Lincoln in County Court. You'll recall I had done one earlier, but with the venue change, which needed to be repeated. It's procedural and will not affect anything."

Millie returned with their drinks and remembered who ordered what, which is always impressive.

When they all had the drinks and Millie had left, Dwight stood and raised his glass. "If I might steal from our host's thunder, I want to thank y'all for being here to aid and support Lincoln and our family through this ordeal. We pray this will be over soon, and we wish our friends from Philly a safe return tomorrow. Y'all have our love and gratitude." They all raised their glasses and clinked each other before sipping.

Sitting down, Dwight added, "Now, before Estelle bursts, pray tell us about your meetings, James and Vernon."

"Me or you?" asked James.

"Me and you; I'll go first. We met Clark Kent at the Dairy Queen, and we all had the M&M Blizzards," Vernon was tantalizing or torturing them, or both. Reaching for his cell phone, he continued, "Mr. Kent was good enough to share these pictures with us. You can take them first, Malcolm, as you'll be most interested. These are pictures of a police vehicle that allegedly hit the Hennessey girl. The first is the vehicle number for identification purposes, and the second shows minor damage to the vehicle where it hits the bike. I emailed these to Vanessa Walker yesterday afternoon."

Malcolm asked, "And may I ask, how did these come into Mr. Kent's possession?"

"You may ask, but he wouldn't tell us. But we can suspect that it was another police officer, or even someone in the garage, who may have been asked to repair the ding. We'll never know."

Malcolm again asked, "Do we know why this Mr. Kent shared this with you?"

"All we know is that Mr. Kent is an FBI agent undercover in Southern Virginia monitoring the KKK and other hate groups. While this was not something the FBI was interested in, I suspect he had a contact in the Emporia PD who thought Kent would know what to do with these pictures."

"Case closed, and the meeting is adjourned. I did a helluva job, didn't I?" Grimsley said with a smile.

Estelle was drying her eyes with her napkin, and Dwight smiled, "This is more than we could have hoped for; our prayers have been truly answered. Need I say thank you again?"

They raised their half-empty glasses again, and Dwight said, "To Clark Kent." They all smiled and yelled, "Cheers."

Vernon said, "There's another tidbit Clark shared with us that may or may not be relevant; he told us that Officer Abbott is a card-carrying member of the KKK. In Philly, a policeperson would be dismissed for belonging to a Hate Group; Malcolm, would you know about Virginia or Emporia?"

"The same here. I'll think about how to use this information best," Grimsley answered.

"And with that, James, you had something to say?"

As Millie appeared, Malcolm interrupted, "How about ordering dinner and perhaps a second drink?"

Dinner orders were placed, and the men all ordered second drinks. Estelle and Beatrice were still nursing their glasses of wine and declined.

James was bursting and took the stage, "My friend here was amazing in our meeting with Dukes. First, he asked him if he still thought Lincoln was guilty, and he said he did. Then he asked if he had it to do over would he do anything differently, and the chief said he might have referred it to the County immediately. Lastly, he asked why he never looked for other suspects, and the chief said no, why would I?

"But the very best., the chief is clearly done answering questions, and we stand, and I need to quote Vernon here, 'Chief, I don't know what's going on here, but you are going to regret the day you arrested Lincoln Anderson."

They all smiled and clapped, raised their glasses again, this time to toast Vernon Brown.

Drinks and a couple of appetizers were served. The main order of business had concluded; the rest of the evening consisted of good food, fellowship, and procedural questions to Malcolm about what they should expect and when. He assured them that tomorrow might be a good day.

At ten after nine, they left with hugs, best wishes, safe travels, and promises to be in touch real soon.

Chapter 53

June 19th, Brookline

It was eighty-thirty when Captain Price convened the daily squad meeting, which would be brief today. He advised everyone of Jeff Newman's death, but they still had no good lead on who may have drugged and raped Kelly Reynolds.

The squad had two other priority cases working and a dozen non-priority. The detectives in charge of each gave any updates they had. Most of them were *nothing new.*

When the meeting was over, Kathy said to Duffy, "I feel bad about not getting back to Newman's wife personally."

"I had the Unis take care of it, Kathy. We can go out there today if you wish to express condolences or ask questions. I suspect she knew little about his drug activity and less about who may have given the roofies to the Reynolds girl. Maybe the less she knows, the better."

"You may be right. Perhaps I'll go by in a day or two. What's next?"

"We'll divide the list of girls, and we'll each call several to confirm they are home. I don't want to run around to all of these not knowing. Let me know when you schedule someone, and I'll do the same."

"Gotcha," Kathy said as Duffy handed her half the list.

Ten minutes later, Kathy got a text from the captain, *please stop in my office.* He probably knew she was still in the office, so there was no sense ignoring it. Hopefully, it would be about the case, but she then thought he would have called Duffy. *Just go already.*

She knocked and entered. "Have a seat, will you?" Price asked. Kathy remained standing.

"What can I do to fix this? I do not want our relationship to end. I care too much for you. Do you want me to get a divorce? Please, Kathy, talk to me." Price was agitated and nervous; Kathy had never seen him lose his cool.

Kathy just stared at him, thinking how to best respond. She wanted to be respectful without giving him any hope of resumption. "Please do not get a divorce on my account, Hank. This is exactly why this was a bad idea from the start. It was destined to end like this. We both need to move on, and with time, I know we both can do it."

"I'll tell you again, Kathy, I'm not certain I can move on, at least with you here. Would you consider a transfer?"

"I should consider a transfer because you can't have me here? I don't think so, Hank. If you wish to pursue a transfer for yourself, I will understand."

"I do not need your approval to transfer you."

"I understand that Captain, but Duffy and I are good, and I think I fit in well with the squad. I have good reviews and no actions against me. After this meeting, I will make a report to IA and our union. I want to keep this civil, Captain, but I will not be bullied."

Kathy walked out, closing his door behind her. She went to her desk, packed her backpack, and whispered to Duffy, "I'm going to see Mrs. Newman." She stepped towards the door, and Duffy said, "Give me a minute to pack up."

She replied, "I'd rather go alone, Duff, thanks." And left the building.

Duffy ran after her and, when he got outside, yelled, "Wait, Kathy!" Kathy slowed down and turned around as Duffy continued his jog towards her. When he caught her, he asked, "What's wrong? Problem with Price?"

"The asshole suggested I transfer out, and if I did not do it voluntarily, he might do it involuntarily."

"Shit! Look, calm down. You want me to talk to him?"

"No, Duff, I do not want you to fight my battles; thanks anyway. I told him I intended to report this incident to IA and the union. Hopefully, that will scare him straight."

"OK, but are you sure you don't want me to go with you to Newman's?"

"Nah! I might play hooky and just go home and take a long bath. Thanks for understanding, Duff. All will be OK."

"I know it will, Kathy, and I've got your back." He extended his arms for a buddy hug, and she accepted it.

Chapter 54

June 20th, Brookline

Detective Richard Duffy was up at his usual time, six-thirty. His normal routine was a shower, shave, and dress, and then have a toasted bagel and his first cup of coffee while perusing email, sports, and news headlines. Lastly, he'd check the department's hotline for overnight updates.

But the sports and news would not get read this morning. He had an email with a video attachment flagged by Gmail with a caution: *THIS SENDER IS NOT IN YOUR CONTACTS; USE CAUTION IN OPENING ATTACHMENTS.*

Throwing caution to the wind, he opened the video. There was no audio, and it showed a teenage boy and girl walking hand in hand into a pool house. *Holy Shit*, Duffy exclaimed to himself—*the friggin smoking gun.*

He hit *KATHY* on his cell, but the call went right to voicemail. He left a message, "Where are you? Get to the office ASAP; I've got the smoking gun."

Duffy put his coffee into a paper cup with a lid, wrapped the bagel in a paper towel, and was out the door. On the way to the station, he left the same message on Captain Price's phone. He put his blue flasher on top of the car, but out of respect for the time, he left the siren off.

He pulled into the station twenty minutes later, a new record for him. The captain's car was in, but Kathy would still need at least fifteen, maybe twenty minutes. He rushed to Price's office, knocked, and, not waiting for an answer, rushed in. Price was sitting at his desk smiling. *He never smiles in the morning*, Duffy thought to himself.

"Dare I ask, what the hell are you smiling about?" Duffy asked.

"I'm smiling about the possibility that you and I are in possession of the same video."

"Mine was sent to me anonymously; how about yours?"

"I got mine from the Chief of Security at Duke University. The basketball coach gave it to him at seven o'clock last night."

"I think we need to get it authenticated before we act on it, agree?"

"I do, and I did; I sent it to Willis last night, and he called me at seven this morning to confirm he cannot find any tampering or anything to suggest it's not authentic," Price said.

"Did you get arrest warrants? When Kathy arrives, I'd like to go out and arrest Longenecker. Can you arrange for a couple of Unis to arrest Friedlander and Bender?"

"Yep, we'll coordinate timing so no one can call the other. Here's the Longenecker warrant."

"I guess we'll have plenty of time to speculate later where the video came from, huh? My guess, though, is our mystery girl."

"I agree and add that we may never know."

Duffy stood to leave and added, "I've always said, Cap, it's better to be lucky than smart."

Price smiled in agreement. "Call into the command center to coordinate the arrests. Thanks, Duff!"

When Duffy got back to his desk, Kathy had just arrived and was unpacking. "Stop right there, young lady. Pack up, we're going out to make an arrest," Duffy barked.

"Huh? What?" Kathy said, turning around to Duffy. "Is this got something to do with your smoking gun?"

"You bet your sweet butt; I'll explain in the car."

They got into Duffy's car, and he queued up the video on his phone. He handed it to Kathy and took off. Kathy hit PLAY on the video and watched in silence until the undressing started, and then exclaimed, "Holy Shit!"

"Can't you come up with anything more original than Holy Shit, Kathy? That's been done to death this morning."

"Where'd this come from?"

"I got this one this morning, and not coincidently, Price also got one last night. Mine came anonymously, and his came from Duke University."

"And we are on our way to arrest Tyler Longenecker?"

"Yep, and two cars of Unis are on their way to arrest Bender and Friedlander. We'll coordinate the arrests when we are all set."

"I hope Daddy Longenecker is there, that smug piece of shit, so that I can hear all of his legal bullshit."

"How do you really feel, Kathy? Don't hold back." They both smiled.

"Are we assuming they both came from our mystery girl? She might have saved two lives had she given us these earlier."

"For now, we are assuming it was her, but I'm not certain we'll continue searching. That's the Captain's call. You're right. Warner would have been arrested with his partners in crime. I'm not certain that Newman would still not have killed himself when Warner was arrested."

They stopped a block away from the Longenecker home. Kathy called into the command center and was told that the car on its way to Benders was still five minutes out.

"Did Price say anything about me?"

"No, but I suspect he knows you told me, and he would be cautious. Do you have any further thoughts?"

"I typed up my complaint last night but did not send it. I wanted to ask your opinion before pulling the trigger. Am I digging a hole I won't be able to escape from?"

"I think you need to make the preemptive move, Kath. If he puts you in for an involuntary transfer, any complaint you make would appear to be defensive. I doubt this will be held against you either by the rank and file or leadership. Do it, and don't look back."

The command center announced that all teams were in place and to proceed with the arrests. Duffy drove up to and entered the Longenecker driveway. He parked, and they walked to the door.

Mrs. Longenecker answered the door and recognized Duffy and Flanagan at once. She opened the door for them and said, "Come in, detectives. How can I help you?"

They stepped into the foyer, and Duffy said, "Good morning, Mrs. Longenecker. We are here to see Tyler."

"Oh, he's still sleeping."

"You'll need to wake him, please. And have him throw on some clothes."

She seemed a bit flustered but turned to go upstairs. With that, Everett Longenecker appeared and, approaching them, asked, "What this time, detectives? You want to know what Tyler had for dinner?"

"Something like that," Duffy replied, enjoying keeping Daddy in the dark.

After a painful two minutes in silence, Tyler appeared with his mom. Kathy removed a pair of handcuffs and stepped towards Tyler.

Tyler Longenecker, I am arresting you for the Involuntary Manslaughter of Kelly Reynolds, the possession and administering of illegal substances, and obstruction of justice. You have the right to remain silent. Anything you say can and will be used against you in a court of law. You have the right to an attorney. If you cannot afford an attorney, one will be provided for you. Do you understand the rights I have just read to you? With these rights in mind, do you wish to speak to me?

Tyler hung his head and remained silent. Mrs. Longenecker screamed and started crying hysterically. Mr. Longenecker said curtly, "This is bullshit, detectives. Let me see your warrant."

Duffy handed it to him and watched while he read it. He returned it to Duffy and turned to Tyler. "Don't say a word to them, Tyler. We'll meet you at the station, and I'll have a lawyer with me. Everything will be fine."

Duffy and Flanagan led Tyler out to the car and put him in the back.

Mrs. Longenecker closed the door and turned to her husband, "Did you know about this?"

"Know about what, the arrest or the crime?"

"The crime. He did it, didn't he?"

"I'm sure he did."

Chapter 55

July 2nd, Northern Virginia

James and Vernon wanted to get an early start for their four-hour drive back to Philadelphia. They knew they could not beat Washington, DC traffic but thought they might hit there after the worst of the morning rush hour. They had a light breakfast in the hotel and hit the road at seven-thirty. That should have them in the DC area between ten and eleven.

Even though they knew they would get a call from the Andersons if any news broke in Emporia, they decided to stream VPM, the Richmond NPR affiliate.

It was nine-forty, and they were getting close enough to DC that they opted for the *EasyPass Lanes* on I-95 when the commentator mentioned, "We have a breaking report from Emporia, Virginia. Reporting live from the Greensville County Courthouse is Diane Witherspoon of WKTR TV. Diane, what do you have?"

Thank you, Michele. In a shocking development, Greensville County Attorney Vanessa Walker has announced that charges against teenage basketball Phenom Lincoln Anderson have been dropped. Anderson had been arrested and charged with Involuntary Manslaughter in the death of Vicky Hennessey on June 25th. Anderson had claimed he had simply seen Hennessey's bike on the road and stopped to see if he could help. His arrest set off a large demonstration by the Black Community here in Southern Virginia and a counter-demonstration by the KKK and Oath Keepers.

Walker also announced the arrest of Officer Jerome Abbott for Involuntary Manslaughter and several related charges in his role as an Emporia Police Officer. Abbott was the one who had hit Vicky Hennessey's bike, allegedly under the influence. He left her dead at the side of the road and then responded to the 9-1-1 call and falsely arrested Anderson.

It was also learned that Abbott is known as Captain Jones of the local Oath Keepers chapter.

Lastly, Michele, Emporia Police Chief Walter Dukes was placed on administrative leave with the intent to dismiss. It is alleged that Dukes knew of the false arrest and covered it up to protect Abbott. Vanessa Walker said that it is possible that charges will be brought against Dukes.

Walker further said that the County would bring in outside authorities to review the leadership and operations of the Emporia Police Department.

From Emporia, Virginia, Diane Witherspoon of WKTR TV.

James turned off the radio and extended his fist to Vernon for the return bump.

"It's a good day for the good guys, Vernon, my friend."

Epilogue

Debbie Gibson drove up to Cambridge, Massachusetts, picked up coffee and a bagel, and entered the Harvard Public Library. She opened her laptop and placed her cell phone next to it. She had already set up a Blur *account for security but still wanted to be away from Brookline for this next step.*

Debbie had much to reflect on...

I always knew that Tyler was a pompous asshole. He was a good-looking guy, a popular jock, and we did have some fun, but by the time we graduated, I was sick of him and hearing about his scholarship to Duke.

I was sure that his dancing at the graduation party with Kelly Reynolds was for my benefit, to let me know he could still attract the hottest chick in school. But I totally did not give a shit and felt a little bad for Kelly, knowing she was being used for something.

I'll never know why I followed them outside and then down to the pool cabana. I knew that Tyler's plan was to hook up, but I wasn't as sure that Kelly was on board for that or that she was that drunk. But filming it was a reflex; I wasn't sure I could watch it. Then later, when I saw Sheldon, Nate, and Billy go in to join them, I was scared shitless. I decided to go around and look for a spot to see inside.

I was haunted by my inability or decision not to intercede when I saw Kelly passed out and the guys undressing her. I actually feared for my safety, as these kids were all drunk and out of control. When they ran out, I thought the best I could do was alert a staff person to Kelly's presence in the pool house. I promptly left the party after telling that server.

When Kelly died, I realized I now held evidence of a murder. What could or should I do with it? I knew I could not keep this to myself.

Then Shelly got murdered. The whole school knew he was selling drugs, so that the heat would have come down on him for sure. Maybe he would have confessed and given up the others. We'll never know. I still think it is possible that Tyler killed Shelly.

But this is it! It wasn't difficult to get the email address of the Duke Coach and the detective handling the case. There was also a police hotline email address where you could send leads or evidence. Between these three, the truth will be exposed.

I'll give it another day or two before dropping it on Instagram.

Thank God this is over.

Brookline

Detective Captain Richard Price was suspended for thirty days with the intention to terminate for his third sexual harassment charge. Further actions were still to be considered.

After being provided with revealing pictures by a Private Investigator, Lindsay Longenecker filed for divorce from her husband.

December 2nd, Richmond Virginia

It takes a lot to get me off Hilton Head Island in December.

But it was December 2nd, and I was only going as far North as Richmond, Virginia. Richmond Commonwealth University was opening its 2022-2023 basketball season against its cross-state rival, George Mason University. In addition to the players' ticket allotment, Coach Blackwell offered me four tickets. After confirming with Dwight Anderson to see if he needed more tickets, I told the coach I only needed three. I had invited Satchel Abney to come over from Newport News, and he was bringing his wife, Shanelle.

I made a reservation for fifteen people in a private room at *The Tobacco Company,* one of my favorite spots in Richmond. The nose count was thirteen, but if an extra couple of people showed, we were good. Fortunately for us old people, the game was at four and should have been over no later than seven. I was counting on it.

Dwight mentioned that his wife's uncle from Philly and the detective who went down to Emporia to help with Lincoln's arrest in the summer were both bringing their wives.

I made hotel reservations for myself and Satch at the Downtown Marriott within walking distance of *The Tobacco Company*. Dwight said his contingent did not need a hotel as they planned to return to Emporia after dinner.

Mellowing just a bit with age, I only got to the arena a half hour before the game rather than my usual hour. The arena was half full by then, but they expected a sell-out in the six thousand-seat arena. I went down to my seat, and my protege, Satch, was sitting in the seat next to mine. I hugged him and Shanelle.

We were in the second row behind the RCU bench. Ten minutes later, Dwight and Estelle Anderson came in with their contingent. They were all sitting in front of us. Hugs and introductions ensued.

The teams came out for their pre-game warm-up. Coach Blackwell made it over to us, greeted the Andersons, and then came up to me and Satch. He thanked us both again and said, "Did your son tell you we became customers of Future Stars?" I smiled, and he winked. One is never too old to make new friends.

I whispered in Estelle's ear, "How did Lincoln seem?"

"He appeared OK, Goldy, but I can assure you he's bursting inside. We all are still finding this hard to believe. I'm so glad you and Satch are here."

"We are too, believe me."

The seats were full now, warm-ups had ended, and the line-ups were announced. I love to look into the eyes of players at this moment. I liked what I saw in Lincoln's.

The game started, and RCU got the ball. It appeared Coach Blackwell liked my advice and was playing Lincoln at guard, the way the Lakers did with Magic Johnson. Lincoln passed the ball into the post, then broke off behind a pick, and when the ball returned to him, he shot. Three-nothing, RCU. Making that first shot always relieves the pressure.

It was a good game. RCU led throughout, but GMU was a solid team and stayed close. Lincoln showed everyone what Satch Abney and I saw back in February. He finished with thirty-four points, twelve rebounds, and eight assists as RCU bested GMU 82-69.

Dwight and Estelle were not certain if Lincoln could or would join us for dinner, so we decided to wait for the team after the game. The players all came out together forty-five minutes later. Lincoln found us all and started hugging everyone. After the family, he came up to Satch and me and hugged us both. "I'll never be able to thank you guys enough, but I will never forget what you have done for me. I love you guys."

If you're lucky in life, you get to have a moment or two like this.

THE END

AUTHOR'S NOTES

If you read my notes at the end of *THE PHENOM*, I said that book was the one I had in me thirty years ago. In reality, THE PHENOM and RECRUITING MURDER are a hybrid of that long-dormant novel.

I'm a Philly guy but a lifelong fan of the Boston Celtics. If there was more than one, I have not found him or her as yet. I have often been asked to justify this since the Celtics were the arch-rivals of Philadelphia's Warriors and then the Seventy-Sixers. It seemed simple to me; here I was in the fifties and sixties, a short, white guard. Who else except Bob Cousy could I emulate?

And let's not forget, Wilt Chamberlain went to Overbrook High School ten years before me and played for the Sixers versus Bill Russell's Celtics. It was a long time before I could appreciate Wilt's greatness.

The meeting and partnering with Red Auerbach were natural and played into the script. I, of course, am vicariously, Lenny Goldstein. But I never coached or scouted, so the story is clearly not autobiographical.

My gratitude to Charlie Serra, a Hilton Head friend who reviewed the manuscript and had his hands full with edits, suggestions, and corrections. Thank you, Charlie.

I hope you have enjoyed this story, and I thank you so much for buying it. If you would be kind enough to leave a positive review on Goodreads or the site where you bought the book, I would sincerely appreciate it. Reviews really matter to independent authors like me.

I'd love to hear from you; feel free to write to me at FrankLazScribe@gmail.com or connect with me on social media.

https://franklazscribe.wixsite.com/frank-lazarus—autho[1]
https://linktr.ee/franklaz
All the Best!
Frank Lazarus

---

1. https://franklazscribe.wixsite.com/frank-lazarus--autho

About the Author

Frank Lazarus was born and raised in West Philadelphia and attended Overbrook High School; after two years in the Army, he obtained his BA Degree from St. Joseph's University in Philadelphia.

He was in the Financial Services and Life Insurance industry for fifty-three years before he retired at the end of 2021.

Frank has three adult children and five grandchildren.

Frank and his partner Deb spend their time on Hilton Head Island and Philadelphia.

Read more at https://franklazscribe.wixsite.com/ frank-lazarus--autho.